CANDY

Scholastic Children's Books
An imprint of Scholastic Ltd
Euston House, 24 Eversholt Street, London, NW1 1DB, UK
Registered office: Westfield Road, Southam, Warwickshire, CV47 0RA

First published in the UK by Scholastic Ltd, 2018

ISBN 978 1407 18427 2

A CIP catalogue record for this book
is available from the British Library.

Typeset in Bembo by M Rules
Printed by CPI Group (UK) Ltd, Croydon, CR0 4YY

Papers used by Scholastic Children's Books are made
from wood grown in sustainable forests.

1 3 5 7 9 10 8 6 4 2

www.scholastic.co.uk

Lavie Tidhar

CANDY

SCHOLASTIC

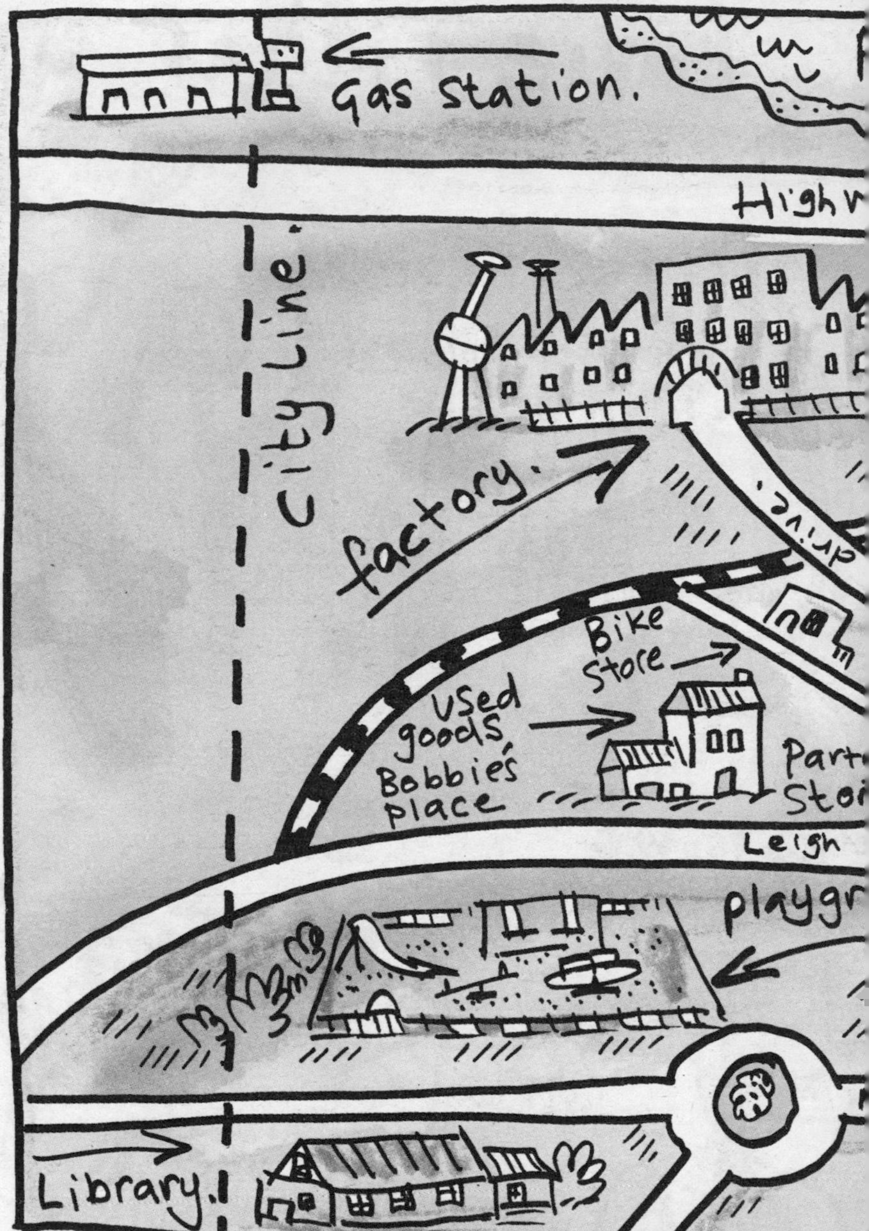

Gas Station.

Highw

City Line.

factory.

drive.

Bike
Store

Used
goods,
Bobbie's
place

Part
Stor

Leigh

playgr

Library.

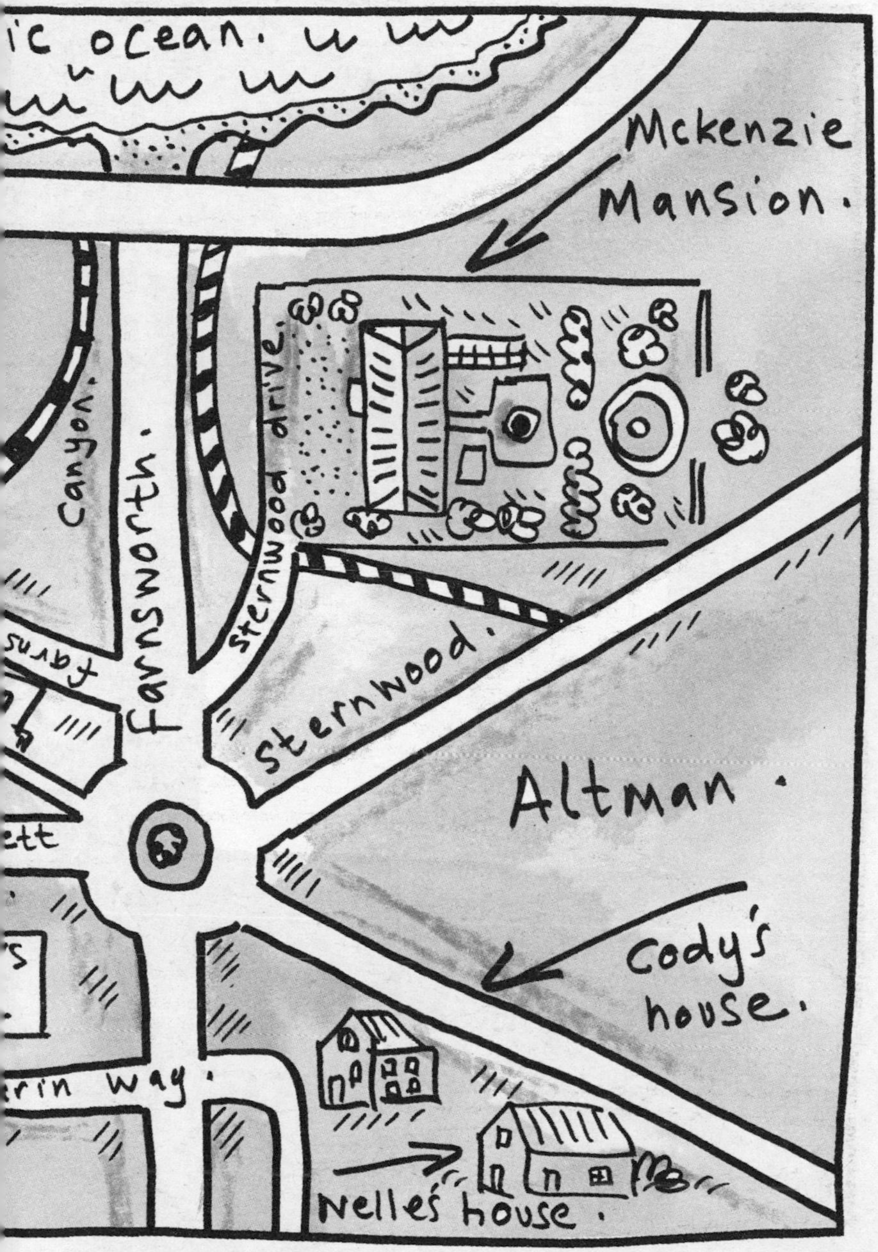

ic ocean.

Mckenzie
Mansion.

canyon.

farnsworth.

sternwood drive.

farns

sternwood.

Altman.

ett

Cody's
house.

rin way.

Nelle's house.

1

The sun was bright through my office window in the backyard of our house. I had a desk and two chairs, one for visitors, a bookcase and a cabinet – everything a private detective's office needs. I also had a box of chocolates in my desk drawer, half-empty or half-full, depending. It was a gift from a grateful client. Like all sweets in the city, it was illegal, but I didn't think anyone would check.

I'd just dipped my hand into the drawer, furtively attempting to select a particular chocolate, trying to feel by touch alone whether it was caramel or marzipan, when there was a knock on the door.

I shut the drawer in a hurry and almost caught my hand in it. I sat up and tried to look busy and competent, like a good private detective should. It'd been a month since school ended for the summer and I'd last had a case. That particular job had brought me up against a notorious bully, Sweetcakes Ratchet and her gang, the Sweetie Pies, and she'd held a grudge ever since. The truth was I was out of pocket money again, I was behind on my luck, my hat was older than I was, and I needed a job even worse than I needed a caramel fudge.

"Come in!" I said.

The door opened and he came in. He had jug ears and red hair and freckles around his nose, and a mouth with too many teeth in it. He was chewing gum openly, like it wasn't illegal. I stared at him. He looked like trouble.

"You're Nelle Faulkner?" he said. "The detective?"

"Depends who's asking," I said. He looked like he was made of cookie dough, rough and unformed. He was about my age, twelve, maybe a little older.

He smiled disarmingly, with all those teeth.

"Your teeth will rot if you keep chewing that gum," I said.

"What are you, my mother?"

I let his attitude fly. It was nothing to me.

"Who are you?" I said.

"I'm sorry, I should have introduced myself."

He wasn't sorry at all. He kept chewing, like his life depended on it.

"I'm Eddie. Eddie de Menthe."

I sat up a little straighter. I knew who he was now.

"You're the candy smuggler?" I said. I'd heard his

name, down the corridors at school. They said he ran half the illegal candy racket in the city. They said if you ever needed a marshmallow or a chocolate button, all you had to do was go see Eddie de Menthe and his gang of candy bootleggers. The bootleggers sold candy under the grown-ups' noses. I didn't know where it came from, and I didn't really care.

"Nah," he said. "It's nothing like that, honest. I'm just a kid."

He didn't look innocent. He looked as wrong as caramel popcorn, and that's about as wrong as you can get.

"So?" I said.

He shrugged like it didn't concern him. "People gotta have candy," he said. "I just help 'em out."

I kind of liked him. He didn't make excuses for himself. But he was trouble and I knew it, and he knew that I knew.

"So how can I help you, Mr de Menthe?" I said.

"Eddie, please."

"If you insist."

"I need a private investigator. A gumshoe." He

smiled. Took out a packet of gum and offered it to me. "Want some?"

"No."

"Ain't a crime," he said.

"Actually, it is."

He chewed and smiled like he didn't care, which I guess he didn't.

"So how can I help you?" I said.

"It's complicated."

"If it's illegal—"

"No, no," he said. "It's nothing like that. I've got . . . people for that."

They said he had every other kid in the city working for him, smuggling in candy and then selling it on. I couldn't imagine what he wanted with me and I told him so.

"Someone stole something of mine," he said. "I need it back."

"Well," I said reasonably. "What did they steal?"

For the first time he looked nervous. "This is just between us, right?" he said.

"We private detectives," I said solemnly, "are

like priests or doctors. Whatever you say stays in this room."

"It's not really a room, though, is it?" he said. "It's a garden shed."

"It's my office."

"But it's a shed," he said. "In your mom's garden. I can see her out the window, weeding the roses."

"Look, buddy," I said, becoming irritated. "You came to *me*. I didn't come to *you*. Where's *your* office, some disused school playground?"

"Actually. . ."

I should have known.

"The one on Malloy Road? Closed down for renovations six months ago?" I said.

"You've never been?" He smirked. "When you go, just make sure you don't lose your marbles."

"What *are* you talking about?"

He kept the smirk on. "You'll see."

I sighed. I sat back and stretched my legs under the desk. I thought about candy. I thought how in other cities they could just buy it in a shop, and we couldn't – not any more. I thought of how good it tasted, and how, just because you make something illegal, doesn't mean it goes away.

"You're avoiding my question," I said.

"Which was?"

"What did you lose?"

"I didn't lose it, I told you. It got stolen."

"What?" I yelled, startling him. He was really beginning to irritate me. "What did you have stolen?"

"It's a teddy, OK?" he said. I drew myself up and looked at him across the table. His eyes were soft and a little sad.

"A teddy?" I said incredulously. Was he joking? He was at least twelve and a *half*.

"A teddy bear. It's an old teddy bear. All right? That's all."

I let the silence linger. He looked uncomfortable, then raised his head and glared at me defiantly.

I said, "Does it have a *name*?"

"Just Teddy."

"That's original."

"It's not mine. It's . . . it belongs to a friend."

"Sure, a friend."

"A *friend*," he said firmly. "And I need it back. It's important."

"Look," I said, "I'm sorry for your loss and all that, but couldn't you just, I don't know, get another one?"

"Did you ever have a teddy?" he said. I squirmed a little uncomfortably and he saw.

"Still got it, right?"

"Her name's Delphina," I said. "Del Bear." I didn't know why I told him that. My dad had bought her for me, when I was small. Before he died.

"I need it back," Eddie de Menthe said.

I stared at him hard. He was one of the most feared candy bootleggers in the whole city, and he was coming to me about a lost teddy bear? Was he serious?

I stared at his face. He did look serious.

No, I thought. It was something worse – he looked *worried*.

"Fine," I said, reaching a decision. I took out my pen and my notepad. "Can you describe it?" I said.

Eddie said, "He's old. He has brown fur that's been

washed too many times so it looks like a dirty grey. He's missing his left eye and there's a patched hole in his chest that looks like a bullet wound that's been sewn shut. He's missing part of his right ear. He's got a cute, black button nose. He has an original label, too faded now to read, but if you could read it, it would say, 'Farnsworth'."

I went still at that name. Eddie watched me closely.

Everyone knew the name. It was etched on the gates of the shuttered factory up on the hill, and on nearly every bar of chocolate that was sold in the city before candy became illegal.

It'd been three long years since Mayor Thornton brought in the great Prohibition Act, banning chocolate and sweets from our city. I was only nine then but I remembered it. We all did. And it was three years since they had closed the factory and Mr Farnsworth had disappeared.

It was getting harder and harder to imagine a world where you could eat chocolate whenever you wanted, in public, or just go to a store and buy it.

Back then the whole city had smelled of it. It was

a smell that rose all over the city, for rich and poor alike, rising day and night from the Farnsworth factory. The smell of chocolate. It was everywhere. It was in our clothes and in our hair and in the warmth of our pillows when we went to sleep at night. I still remembered. It had been my father's smell.

He had worked in the factory and the chocolate was on his skin and under his nails and in his hair. The smell had clung to him, no matter how much he washed, no matter what cologne he used.

It was a part of him.

Now the city just smelled of flowers and trees, of baking bread and coffee and car exhaust fumes and sweat, like any other city.

But it used to smell like a fairy tale.

It used to smell *wonderful.*

I cleared my throat. "What else can you tell me?"

"I can tell you it's important I get it back."

"I charge fifty cents a day plus expenses," I said.

He shrugged, like money was nothing to him, which perhaps it wasn't.

"I need that teddy back," he said.

Gradually I got the rest of the details out of him. He kept the teddy bear in his "office" in the abandoned old schoolyard on Malloy, where kids came for bootleg chocolate and a game of marbles. He thought maybe one of his rivals could have stolen it, but didn't say why he thought that. I had the impression there was rather a lot he wasn't telling me. He said his main rival was a kid called Waffles, who lived up on the hill. I'd never heard of him before. Other than that, he didn't know. But I could see that he was worried.

"I'll make some enquiries," I said at last. "And I'll have to look over your turf too."

"I already told them to expect you," he said.

"All right."

We stared at each other across the desk in silence. Eddie de Menthe was a big boy. He could look after himself. And yet, still, at just that moment, he looked a little lost himself.

"I'll find it," I said.

"Good." He looked relieved. He stood up to go. At the door he turned back to me.

"Thanks, Nelle."

He turned to the door.

"Hey," I said.

"Yeah?"

"Why me?"

For just a moment he smiled, and his face softened.

"We used to dig in the sandbox together," he said.

I looked at him, puzzled. "I don't remember that at all," I said.

"Yeah, well." He shrugged. "See you, Nelle."

"See you, Eddie."

When he left I remained seated. My mother had gone into the house and Eddie sneaked out through the back gate without being seen. He was good at that.

The sun streamed in through the window.

And I thought about chocolate.

2

It sounded like a simple enough case. The sort I'd take any day of the week. It was just a case of a missing teddy bear.

That was something I could handle.

Couldn't I?

But the candy trade wasn't something I'd ever got involved in before. I mean, I wasn't above eating the occasional chocolate bar if it came my way, but mostly I followed the rules.

A photo of my dad hung on the wall near my desk. I looked at it every day and, now, I looked at it again.

In the picture the factory gleamed new in the daylight, the sun shining over the big sign that said, "Farnsworth's Chocolate Factory".

Standing in front of the gates, smiling for the camera, were my mother and father, my father in his blue overalls, my mother in a summer dress. In my father's arms sat a younger me, beaming toothlessly. I liked to imagine I remembered that day: the feel of my father's arms around me, holding me safe, warm, loved. The sun shone on us.

Behind us, the great machines thudded as they worked, day and night, pounding, mixing, blending, conching and tempering. It must have been a family day at the factory, because all around us were other families, other moms and dads who worked there, machinists and wrappers, accountants and tasters.

Sometimes I thought I could still taste the chocolate in the air, and see clouds as fluffy as cotton candy in the big blue sky.

But, of course, I no longer could.

When I went into the garden, my mother was back watering the plants. She pottered about happily,

wearing gardening gloves. Every now and then she'd reach with a finger to remove the damp hair that stuck to her forehead. She smiled when she saw me. I gave her a hug and told her I was going to the playground, and then I unchained my bike and rode off.

It was a hot day, hot with the kind of heat that melted chocolate into sticky puddles. I turned left on to Leigh Brackett Road. It was a pleasant tree-lined street with plenty of shade. From the bakery on the corner I could smell fresh bread. It made me think of doughnuts and chocolate croissants, Danish pastries and éclairs. In my bag all I had was half a cheese sandwich and an apple. It was healthier, anyway. At least that's what the mayor said.

Mayor Thornton had come into our lives like a thief in a candy store. When he ran for mayor it was by telling everyone that all chocolates and sweets had to be banned. For everyone's sakes. For the children. For our *health*. I guess people believed him, because they voted him in.

And when he became mayor, his first order of business was announcing the Prohibition Act.

I could see Mayor Thornton's face everywhere I went, staring at me from the lawn signs in front of the houses I passed. In all the posters he was smiling. He had even, very white teeth. He looked like a man who had never eaten a chocolate bar in his life.

I reached Malloy Road. It was a wide avenue of quiet residential apartments and semi-detached homes, with the old school occupying almost the whole block on the opposite side of the road. It had been rundown for a few years and was now shut for renovations, but there were no builders anywhere and it didn't look like there had been for months. The school was fenced off and there were signs hanging all around, but they were rusted, and the fence itself was full of holes where dogs, maybe, had gone through it. The signs all showed the mayor, smiling as he perched on a crane, wearing a bright yellow hard hat.

The school buildings rose grey-black against the blue sky and their shadow fell like dark chocolate on the road at my approach.

It felt quiet, though the school was not entirely empty. I walked along the fence and around the back, where the playground was. Here the fence had been reinforced, and light wood panels erected so that you couldn't see inside. There wasn't a gate as such, but as I approached I saw a boy and a girl standing guard next to a wooden door.

"Password?"

"Eddie said I could come in. Name's Faulkner. Nelle Faulkner."

They exchanged glances.

"Eddie said to expect you. You can go in."

I looked at the door. I couldn't tell what was behind it.

I was afraid that if I went in, I'd be entering a world I didn't know and didn't understand. And that if I did, I wouldn't be able to get out again. But I was also curious. A part of me *wanted* to know. I didn't like mysteries. It's why I always tried to solve them.

"So? Are you going in or not?"

I stared at the door. Curiosity won, and I nodded. The boy pushed the door open and stood aside to let me pass.

I stepped into the playground.

3

It was a hot day, but the playground was shaded by the school buildings. Inside the enclosure was a hive of activity. There were kids everywhere, lounging on makeshift picnic tables, eating their way through assorted candy, all without a grown-up in sight.

Chalk rings were drawn on the ground, with marbles scattered inside each ring. The objective of the game was to capture the most marbles with your shooter, which was a larger marble. All you had to do was aim your shooter into the ring and try to knock as many marbles out as possible.

It wasn't as easy as it sounds.

Around the players, other kids were betting candy on the winners. No one shouted, but encouragements were whispered intensely as each player took their turn. I saw my neighbour Cody, the little boy from next door. I didn't know Cody came to places like this, and I realized that I didn't like it. Whenever I could, I tried to look out for him.

He was lying on his stomach, with a large pile of marbles beside him. One eye was closed in concentration and he flicked his marble at the ring. It connected with an audible *ping* and several other glassy balls flew in all directions and two left the ring altogether. Another boy went and picked them up and brought them to Cody and he added them to his stash. He was clearly doing well.

Around him there was a murmur of excitement, and I saw sweets changing hands. Cody took his turn again and this time got three marbles out of the ring, including one of his opponents' big shooters. The other player shouted in disappointment and got up, empty-handed. Cody grinned. I watched until the ring was empty and the rest of the players ousted. Cody gathered his winnings into a bag. He was surrounded by admirers who slapped him on the back and ruffled his hair.

He was still grinning, until he saw me.

"Nelle!"

"Hello, Cody."

"You won't tell, will you, Nelle?" he said, looking worried.

"Where's your mom?" I said.

"She's gone to the movies with Stuart."

Stuart was his stepdad.

"You shouldn't be here, Cody."

His face fell. "But I like it," he said. "I just like to play marbles, Nelle. It's something I'm good at."

He looked at me with big dark eyes. He extended his hand. "Here," he said. "Do you want some marbles?"

I had to smile.

"Keep them," I said. "But you're coming home with me."

"All right," he said. He looked at me with eyes full of trust.

"Who's in charge here?" I asked.

"Anouk," he said. "Anouk is."

I looked up. By the wall of the school lounged a dark-haired girl, older than me by a couple of years. She saw me looking and came over, moving with quiet purpose.

"You Faulkner?" she said.

"You must be Anouk."

She ruffled Cody's hair fondly. "Eddie mentioned you might be along. He said to show you to the office."

"If you could."

I turned to Cody.

"You stay here," I said.

"All right, Nelle." His eyes drifted to the game of marbles. I left him and followed Anouk to the office. She led me through a door, into a small storage room.

I looked around me. Boxes of what I assumed to be candy were stacked everywhere. If I'd ever thought about it before, I imagined the candy trade was just a game, a handful of chocolates at a time, but this shocked me – the scale of it was much bigger than

I'd expected. It didn't *feel* so much like a game, all of a sudden.

"Eddie said to tell you the teddy was sitting on that shelf," Anouk said, pointing. It was a shelf over an old desk and it held a variety of random objects, an old trophy and a starfish and a tin decorated with flowers. "I always just assumed it was Eddie's good luck charm, something his mom gave him before she died."

"It was stolen from *here*?" I said, surprised.

Anouk shrugged. "I guess," she said. "Though there is only one door and there's usually someone here."

"And nothing else is missing?"

"Not that I know of."

"That's odd," I said. "You'd think if they'd try to steal anything it'd be the candy."

She shrugged again. "I can't see how the teddy bear could have been stolen," she said. "Not unless it was one of us."

"Was it?"

"No, Nelle," she said patiently. "None of us took the teddy. Besides, what for? It was just an old bear."

I nodded reluctantly. I didn't know how the teddy

was stolen yet, but in order to find it I also had to understand *why* it was stolen. I thought Anouk was wrong to suggest it couldn't have been anyone here. They didn't seem to guard the room all that well, and anyone inside the playground could have used a moment when it wasn't guarded to go in and snatch the teddy.

The *how* of the theft wasn't much of a mystery, in that case. The thief could have easily taken it out of the playground.

But figuring that out didn't get me any closer to finding out who took it.

The real question was *why* it was stolen.

What was so important about an old teddy bear?

It clearly mattered to Eddie . . . mattered more than it should. Could it be anything to do with the candy trade? And if so, was it really wise for me to get in any deeper?

"You want some chocolate?" Anouk said.

"No, thanks." I looked at her, and thought about this playground operation, and all the candy boxes in the storage room.

"Where do you get your chocolate from?" I said.

Anouk gave me a look. "That's not the sort of question you want to be going around asking, Nelle," she said. It sounded like a warning and I left it at that – for the time being, at least.

"Oh, just one more thing," I said at the door.

She turned back to me, not bothering to hide her irritation. "What is it?"

"Eddie mentioned you're rivals with. . ." I consulted my notebook. "Waffles McKenzie?"

"Yeah, he's got his own gang," she said. "He has a place down near Altman Street, back of a used goods store."

"What, Bobbie Singh's place?" I said, surprised.

"Yeah. You know him?"

I nodded. Bobbie was a friend of mine.

"Well . . . anything *else*, detective?"

"No," I said. "Thanks again." And I went to pick up Cody. He was still playing marbles but he got up without complaint when I called him.

We went outside. His hand in mine felt hot and sticky with chocolate. As we crossed the street a black car moved smoothly out of its parking space on the other side of the street, under the trees, swerving ahead of us on the road home.

After I dropped Cody home I set off again. There was an election rally in full swing in Ohls Square as I cycled past. After serving almost a full term, the mayor was running for re-election. It looked festive, with flags and bunting and a stage set up at the centre of the square, near the fountains. A marching band played and balloons decorated the stage. Volunteers handed out carrots and celery sticks, though the people who accepted them mostly did so without any visible enthusiasm.

I stopped and took a glass of beet juice from one of

the volunteers, then regretted it as soon as I took a sip. I saw elderly Mr Lloyd-Williams from the Trinkets, Teddies & Toys Emporium walk past.

"No, thank you, young lady, I do not want a carrot!" he said in his British accent as he was being offered one. "If I'd wanted to eat *vegetables* I would have stayed in England, where at least they have the decency to *boil* them first!" He stomped off in a huff.

There was a tap on a microphone and then a screech of feedback from the speakers in front of the stage. Then Mayor Thornton came on.

"Hello!"

He raised his arms in the air. The crowd broke into applause.

"Everyone having a good time?"

"Yeah!"

More applause. The mayor beamed down on us. From up on the stage he looked benevolent, relaxed.

"Health! Prosperity! Follow your dreams!"

"Yeah!"

"Eat your—"

"Greens!"

"Eat your—"

"Greens!"

"Eat your—"

"G—"

"But, seriously, folks. Thank you for coming. It's been my honour and my privilege to serve as your mayor for the past three years. Prohibition has made our children healthier, happier, and better adjusted for life. Our town is peaceful and prosperous. I won't keep you long – I know you're all busy. In the coming election, please vote." He grinned at us, with those dazzling white teeth. "Vote Thornton for mayor. Can you do that for me? For all of us? For our children, and our children's future?"

The crowd went wild. They threw celery sticks in the air.

"Thornton! Thornton for mayor!"

The mayor raised his arms again, hands clasped together over his head, and beamed at the crowd.

"You've been wonderful!" he said.

The marching band struck up again and balloons

floated into the air. The mayor climbed down to shake people's hands.

I got back on my bike and rode away.

There was a lingering bad taste in my mouth from that one sip of beet juice.

I rode down Altman Street and then turned left back on to Leigh Brackett Road, and stopped outside a store with a sign that said, "Used Goods".

The window was grimy and the display behind it showed mismatched mannequins wearing clothes that must have been old even before I was born. When I pushed open the door, a bell rang.

It was dark and cool inside the store. On the shelves were odds and ends: a pair of ladies' gloves; an old gold coin with a faded handwritten sign next to it that said it was a rare Brasher Doubloon (whatever that was); a stack of dusty crime novels by authors no one remembered any more; the statue of

a black falcon; a silver tea-set creamer in the shape of a hideous cow; an old lighter with an unintelligible inscription; a crystal skull; a packet of Victorian letters; and more, a lot more. There was everything in the store but customers. The things on the shelves could each have once been the deciding clue in some long-ago crime. Now you could buy them and still have change from a dollar.

A man in a turban stood behind the counter.

"Hello, Nelle," he said when he saw me.

"Mr Singh," I said, and then, "is Bobbie in?"

Mr Singh gave a long-suffering sigh and jerked his thumb and said, "In the back."

"Thanks."

"Can't you tell him to go out every now and then, Nelle?" Mr Singh said. "Get some fresh air, play with a ball? He won't listen to me."

"He won't listen to anybody," I said.

Mr Singh nodded mournfully.

"How is Mrs Singh?" I asked. Bobbie's mom was still at the hospital. She had been sick for some time, and I knew how anxious they both were.

"Oh, it's kind of you to ask, Nelle," he said. "But, really, there's no need for you to worry."

It was the sort of thing grown-ups always said. But I nodded all the same.

"How's business?" I said, instead.

"Oh, booming."

I looked around the dark, dusty shop. The shelves with ancient rotted things nobody wanted any more, if they ever had.

"All right," I said.

There was a small door at the back of the shop and I pushed it open, entering a storage room that was attached to the store. Bobbie had dragged in some plastic tables and chairs and a fan moved slowly in a corner pushing hot air around. A long wooden counter lined one side of the room, and it was suspiciously empty.

"Nelle!"

"Hello, Bobbie," I said.

Several kids varying in ages sat around, all staring at me, their hands firmly under the tables, out of sight.

"Nelle's cool," Bobbie said, and they relaxed. The hands came out all holding candy, which they proceeded to shove into their faces. Bobbie grinned at me, then ducked behind the counter and brought out all the stuff he must have hastily pushed underneath when I entered. I stared at the merchandise.

Milk chocolate and dark chocolate and cocoa butter, fruit sours and lemon drops, sprinkles and poppers and whole-nut bars and candied almonds, waffles and bonbons, liquorice and pralines – everything but ice cream.

Of all the things I missed, I missed ice cream the most. My mouth watered just at the thought of a vanilla cone smothered in chocolate sauce. Among the candy I spotted familiar wrappers, all from out of town, from companies like the St Creme-Egge Corporation and Madame Sosotris and the Brothers Soufflé.

Bobbie Singh stood behind the counter. He was a short skinny kid a year older than me, though he looked two years younger.

He was a quiet, hard-working kid. I'd known him since kindergarten.

"Hey, Bobbie, I wanted to ask you some questions," I said.

"Sure, Nelle. But hold on—"

He turned, and so did I, just in time to realize there was someone else in the room.

She loomed over me with an ugly sneer on her face, and stuck her finger at me. "What is *she* doing here?"

I made a face.

"Hello, Sweetcakes," I said.

Her real name was Mary Ratchet, but everybody

called her Sweetcakes. She was a big mean suet of a girl with fists like giant sweet potato pies. I'd run up against her on my last case, her and her crew of girls, the Sweetie Pies. Though there was nothing sweet about her or her crew.

We were in the same class at school together. Now she leered at me with teeth that had seen too much candy pass through them. "Looking for trouble, *detective*?"

She still held a grudge. She was the sort of person to hold on to a grudge like chewing gum stuck to a shoe. The last time I'd run up against her, it was on a case that was unrelated to chocolate. I'd got the better of her that time, and she hadn't liked it, not one bit.

"Looking for Bobbie," I said pleasantly. "If you don't mind. . .?"

"But I *do* mind," she said, advancing on me, those pie fists swinging by her side. "Sweetcakes *minds*, that a low-down dirty *gum*shoe shows her face round here."

I stood and faced her calmly, though my heart was racing. She was bigger and meaner than me, and she had backup. Three of her girls, Daisy and Rosie and

Little May, stood behind her, glaring at me. The kids around the tables didn't even bother to look up. They were munching on chocolate buttons as though their lives depended on it.

"I'm not here for you," I said.

"Oh, *aren't* you?"

"Cool it, Sweetcakes," Bobbie said. His voice was quiet but it carried.

Sweetcakes stood and looked at me with that same ugly sneer. "This ain't over, gumshoe," she said.

"I look forward to catching up again," I said. I kept my face blank.

"Soon," Sweetcakes said.

"Any time!" I said.

She licked chocolate stains from the corners of her lips. "I'll be seeing you, Bobbie. I'll be seeing you real soon. Come on, girls," she said. She went past me and as she did her shoulder slammed into mine, hard, and I stumbled. She laughed, and her girls laughed with her. Then they all left.

"I'm sorry about that, Nelle," Bobbie said.

"What was that about?" I said, brushing myself off.

"It's complicated."

"Can we talk?"

"In the back."

I followed him behind the counter. A small door was set into the wall and he opened it.

It was really not much more than a cupboard. There were bags of chocolate coins and trays of creme eggs and half-opened crates filled with chocolate bars in plain wrappers. A bare light bulb hung from the ceiling and the walls were unvarnished. I perched on a crate.

"So this is it?" I said. I'd suspected before, but didn't know for sure. "You sell candy?"

"It's just a bit of chocolate," Bobbie said defensively.

"Where do you get it from?" I said.

He gave me a look. "What is this about, Nelle?"

"Just satisfying my curiosity," I said.

"Curiosity can be a dangerous thing."

I shrugged. "I like to live dangerously."

Bobbie sighed.

"So come on, spill. I heard you get your candy from Waffles."

"Why all the questions, Nelle?"

"Job," I said. "Missing teddy bear. Know anything about that?"

"What?" he said, looking confused. "Why would I?"

I shrugged. "You tell me."

"I don't know anything about a teddy bear, Nelle."

"Know anything about Eddie de Menthe?"

He went still. "I got no trouble with Eddie. What's this about?"

I shook my head, gave him a tight smile. "I prefer to ask the questions, Bobbie."

"What's in it for me?" he said.

"I thought we were friends."

"We *are* friends, Nelle. That's why I haven't kicked you out yet."

"Come on, Bobbie. Help me out," I said. "What am I getting myself into?"

"I don't know about no missing teddy bear of Eddie's," he said, "but there could be some trouble coming, so that might be connected."

He sighed.

"Sometimes I feel like I've been playing a game that was supposed to be fun," he said, "only it's been going for too long and it isn't fun any more, and all the other players won't let you quit."

"I don't even know the game," I said.

"Oh, you look like you'll catch on quickly."

"So can you fill me in?"

"Are you sure you *want* me to, Nelle? It ain't too late to back off yet."

Was I sure?

Like I said, I was curious. Being curious could get you in trouble. But being curious could get you anywhere.

I nodded. "Sure," I said.

"*Fine.* There are three major players in the candy trade right now," Bobbie said. He ticked them off on his fingers: "You already know Eddie de Menthe. He runs the biggest gang, the Cookie Dough Boys. Then there's Waffles. His gang ain't much smaller. He runs everything, including my place. He does candy, but what he really loves are pastries. He's got the market cornered on that. You ever want a freshly-baked cinnamon swirl or a jam doughnut, then Waffles is your boy."

I filed it away. "Who's the third?" I said.

And why did I get a bad feeling?

Eddie gave me a sad little smile. "Didn't you figure it out, Nelle? I'm surprised at you."

He nodded at the door. "After all, she was just here," he said softly.

Then I understood what he was trying to tell me and I felt sick, as though I'd had one too many biscuits.

"Sweetcakes," I said.

He inched his head in reply.

"She's trying to muscle in on your place?" I said.

"She's a big girl with even bigger dreams."

"The Sweetie Pies?"

"Yes. They've been causing trouble for the past month, ever since school broke up for the summer. This visit, just now? She's been leaning on me to work for her. Or else."

"Or else what?"

He was about to speak when we heard shouts behind the door – and my question was unexpectedly and unpleasantly answered.

5

When we pushed open the door, we were welcomed with a scene of chaos.

Multi-coloured smoke filled the room, of the sort you got in any joke shop, and it was mixed with a stench that made my eyes water. Panicked kids tried to escape but couldn't see where they were going, and ran into each other and into the furniture. The room smelled like someone had let a skunk in. Cries of panic rose into the air. Chairs fell over. In the nightmarish smoke, figures moved like shadows. A horrific figure, face covered in a red-and-pink polka dot bandana,

appeared out of the smoke. Sweetcakes.

Before I could react she disappeared back into the smoke. I tried to breathe but there was no air, just the smell of rotten eggs and sewers.

It was *horrible*. Someone had set off a smoke bomb and mixed it in with a stink bomb or two just for the hell of it. And by *someone*, I thought, I really meant Sweetcakes Ratchet. Clearly, she and the Sweetie Pies hadn't intended to leave Bobbie with just a friendly chat.

"Come on!" I said, grabbing Bobbie by the arm. My eyes were watering from the stink. "You've got to open the door and let some air in!"

He was coughing. The smoke came blue and green and yellow. I pulled him with me and tried the door back to the shop but it was locked and I heard Sweetcakes laughing somewhere behind me.

"The back door!" Bobbie said. Together, we staggered round the room, bumping into things, feeling our way by touch. It was hard to see. Bobbie kept coughing beside me. Where was the back door? There had to be a door, for deliveries. As far as I remembered it opened on to a small alleyway that was rarely in use.

At last I found it. I pushed the door open and for a moment cool, clean air rushed into the room. Then the rest of the Sweetie Pies shoved me out of the way and ran outside, laughing. Their arms were full of Bobbie Singh's contraband candy bars. They'd taken the lot.

I fell on the floor and saw Sweetcakes stand over me, laughing behind her bandana. The red and pink polka dots made me think of chewed bubblegum.

"You tell Waffles McKenzie this is going to be *my* candy store!" she said. "You tell him I said so!" And she laughed uproariously and vanished into the alleyway outside. In moments she was gone.

I sat there as the rest of the kids staggered past me into the clean air, their faces still smudged with chocolate. The air smelled of stink bomb and candy. It was a smell I wouldn't forget in a hurry.

The Sweetie Pies had made their point.

I went back to Bobbie. He was standing in the

middle of the room looking at the mess when Mr Singh came in.

Bobbie cried, "Dad!" and ran to him.

"What is this?" Mr Singh said. He looked bewildered and angry. "Why was there a chair jammed under the door? What were you kids playing in here? What is that *smell*?"

"Dad, where *were* you?"

"I got an urgent call," Mr Singh said. "To go to the hospital. I didn't want to worry you. But when I got there it turned out to be someone's idea of a joke."

Bobbie and I exchanged glances.

Sweetcakes.

"It was just someone pulling a prank," Bobbie said. "It's all right. How's Mom?"

"She's ... fine." Mr Singh looked awkward. "She'll get better, Bobbie." He gave him a quick hug, then let go.

"Well, clean up this mess," Mr Singh said. "Then, you know ... go outside, Bobbie. Play with a ball. Always inside. . ." He shook his head.

"Bobbie, I still need to talk to you," I said.

"Not now, Nelle."

"OK," I agreed soberly. "Not now."

I squeezed his shoulder briefly, and turned to go.

I felt shaken. Once outside, I took a deep breath of the warm, fresh air. The sun was setting but it was still light.

My investigation had barely even started and already I found myself in the midst of a turf war between gangs. That the gangsters were twelve years old made no difference. I went to get my bike and saw someone had kicked it savagely, and the spokes on the front wheel were bent. It was Sweetcakes and the Sweetie Pies again, no doubt.

I rubbed the bridge of my nose. It had been a long day. A black car was parked across the street and when I looked, the engine started and it glided away into the night. For a moment I had the feeling that I'd seen it before, but it must just have been my imagination.

I took the bike and began wheeling it on the long walk home.

6

When I got home I went straight up to my mom and gave her a big hug. She fussed over me and made me feel better. I told her I'd gone to visit Bobbie and there was a fight. I really wanted to tell her about it, and what I'd found out, and that I was anxious, but I didn't want to worry her.

"Are you *sure* you're all right?" she said, but I didn't answer.

Later, she tucked me into bed. I felt queasy from the stink bomb and the smoke. My mind swirled with unanswered questions. Why was the teddy bear taken from Eddie's playground? Did one of his rivals have it stolen? But, again, it made no sense – why would anyone steal an old teddy bear? And why did it say Farnsworth on it?

It took me a long time to fall asleep.

In the morning, the sun shone through the window and the new day smelled of cut grass and fried eggs. The cut grass was outside. The eggs were in the kitchen, and they were for me.

After breakfast my mom went to work and I was alone. I went outside to my office. As I approached it, I saw that the door was ajar. I was sure I had locked it the previous night, with the rusty padlock my dad used when it was his tool shed. I always did. Not that there was anything worth stealing inside.

Cautiously, I pushed the door open.

My office lay in ruins. Someone had gone through everything, pulling out my files, spreading them across the floor. The desk drawers had been torn out and emptied, and the desk lay on its back with its legs in the air like a wounded animal. Someone had found the box of candy and upended it on the floor and then

stepped on the chocolates until they made an icky pool of sweet-smelling goo on the floor.

I stood there, horrified.

Someone had gone through my office, searching. But for what? I had nothing worth stealing, and nothing I could see was missing.

I was shaken. I stood in the doorway and looked at the mess.

Was it connected with Eddie de Menthe's visit? It must have been.

But I didn't understand why. I still had no answers. I felt angry and confused that someone would do this. What were they looking for? There was nothing important in my office. I took a deep breath and tried to calm myself down, and got to work.

I spent the morning trying to sort out the damage. I cleaned the floor and put the desk back up and straightened the hatstand and put away the files, in order. It made me feel better.

Whoever had broken in had even taken down the photo of my dad I kept on the wall by the bookcase. They'd taken a knife to the back of it, searching to see if something was hidden inside the frame. I carefully took out the picture and was relieved it hadn't been damaged.

My books lay about everywhere. They had even turned them upside-down to see if I'd hidden anything inside the pages. Bookmarks and pressed leaves, a postcard from an aunt I didn't remember receiving, and a foreign note in a currency I didn't recognize. Each one could have been a clue but wasn't. It was just stuff.

As I stacked up the books again, I wondered what I had let myself in for, agreeing to help Eddie de Menthe. It was clear he hadn't been honest with me. He had made it sound like a simple case of a missing teddy, but it was obviously something more. Someone *really* wanted to find that bear, but I still had no idea why anyone would care about it, or who would want to steal one. Either way, I needed to question Eddie again.

When I stepped outside I saw a small curly-haired head pop over the fence and then quickly disappear.

"Cody?" I said. "Is that you?"

The head reappeared. Two solemn eyes regarded me over the fence.

"Hello, Nelle," he said shyly. "Are you all right?"

"Yes, Cody, I'm fine."

He worried at his bottom lip with his teeth. "It's

only that. . ." he said, and stopped.

"It's OK, Cody. You can tell me."

"It's only that they came last night," he said. "I saw them come in through the gate. They were quiet. They opened the door and went inside, so I thought it was all right. I thought they must be friends of yours."

"I'm sure they were," I said reassuringly. "Did you get a good look at them?"

"No, it was dark. I only saw shadows."

"How many of them were there?"

"Two," he said. He thought about it. "Just two."

"Boys? Girls?"

He thought about it some more. He was a serious kid. He liked to give each question the consideration it deserved.

"I couldn't see," he said at last, and I felt disappointment, but I didn't want to show it. "It was too dark. I'm sorry, Nelle."

"That's OK, Cody."

"It was weird, though," he said. "Are you sure they were friends of yours, Nelle?"

"Why do you ask that, Cody?"

"It's only, they were grown-ups."

"What?"

"They were grown-ups," he repeated. "I don't know why they came to your office, Nelle."

"I don't either, Cody," I said. I felt hollow inside.

Grown-ups?

That couldn't be right.

Could it?

"Do you have any candy, Nelle?" he asked. Still numb from the shock, I put my hand in my pocket. My fingers closed on something round and hard. I pulled it out.

It was a mint.

I had no idea what it was doing there.

"Here."

He looked at it dubiously, then his hand darted out and took it from my palm. His fingers were hot and sticky. "Thanks, Nelle," he said, without enthusiasm.

"Lay off the sweets, Cody."

He smiled at that. "But I like them, Nelle. Well, see you."

"See you, Cody."

His head disappeared. I leaned against the fence, breathing hard. I didn't see how anything added up. A missing teddy, rival gangs selling illegal candy, and now someone had ransacked my office, except they weren't kids, they were *adults*.

What were they *looking* for?

I was scared, but that didn't mean I was going to back off. My dad used to say I was stubborn, and he didn't always mean it in a positive way. But I knew it was a good thing I *was* stubborn. I wasn't going to drop the case. Not this quickly.

First things first, Eddie de Menthe and I needed to have a serious talk.

I left the house on foot. It was a hot day, the sort of day when you crave an ice cream, but that just wasn't an option. It'd been three long years since I'd heard an ice cream van go past, blaring its tune.

I was headed back to the abandoned schoolyard on Malloy Road where Eddie had his base of operations, but I didn't make it.

Maybe it was the heat, or still being upset about my

office, but I didn't see them until they were almost on top of me, and by then it was too late.

7

"You Nelle Faulkner?"

"Depends," I said. "Who wants to know?"

There were two of them, boys I didn't recognize, a year or two older than me.

The one on the left looked like he'd always had too much chocolate. The one on the right, by contrast, looked like he always ate all of his greens.

The one on the left looked at his nails. "She's got a smart mouth," he complained, seemingly to no one.

"You the gumshoe?" the skinny one said. "The private eye?"

They didn't scare me, but it paid to be cautious.

"What do you want?" I said.

"We're looking for Nelle Faulkner," the thin one said.

"The detective," the big one said.

"Never heard of her," I said.

The big one nodded with that same slow sadness. "Only you look a lot like her," he said.

"Who are you?" I said.

"I'm Ronny," the thin one said.

"I'm Gordon," the big one said.

"Well, it was *very* nice to meet you," I said, taking a step back. "But I really gotta run."

Somehow, Gordon stayed ahead while Ronny snuck up behind me. I was trapped between them.

"What's your hurry?"

"Get back!" I shouted.

"Whoa, whoa," Gordon said, raising his hands. "You got us all wrong, Nelle. We just wanted to invite you."

"To come with us," Ronny said.

"Come with you *where*?" I said.

"To a birthday party," Gordon said – as if it were obvious.

"There'll be ice cream and cake," Ronny said. "And waffles."

"Wait," I said. "You work for Waffles?"

"Boss wants to see you."

"Boss wants to have a chat."

"He sent you an invite," Gordon said, with a sour expression. He reached into his suit pocket and brought out a card and handed it to me.

"I didn't get a card," Ronny said. He sounded disappointed.

I looked at the card. It was heavy cream paper, and the lettering was done by hand. It said:

You are cordially invited

To

Elmore McKenzie's

13th Birthday Party

Looking forward to seeing you there!

"*Elmore*?" I said. "Waffles's name is *Elmore*?"

"You gotta problem with that?" Gordon said.

"But *Elmore*?"

"Boss doesn't like people making fun of his name."

I waved the invitation. "He wants me to come to his *party*?"

"His birthday party."

"And we're gonna be late."

"There's going to be *cake*," Gordon said. His big moist eyes seemed to beg me not to argue.

"Chocolate cake," Ronny said. "With sprinkles and frosting and icing and cream and, like, *walnuts*."

"All right, enough!" I said. They were giving me a headache.

"So you'll come?"

"Is it far?"

"He lives on Sternwood Drive," Ronny said.

I whistled. "Up on the hill?"

"Sure."

I made up my mind. I had been planning to see Waffles, anyway. He had simply jumped to the front of the queue.

"Lead the way, boys," I said.

And so, accompanied by Waffles's two goons, I went to a party.

8

Sternwood Drive twisted its way up the hillside like a long string of liquorice. On a clear day you could see out as far as Bay City. The sea below was blue and calm and in the sky above clouds floated like candyfloss. Beyond, the city sprawled, but what dominated the view and drew the eye was the hulking outline of the chocolate factory, standing proud and alone on Farnsworth Drive on the opposite hill. I stared at it as we walked up to the gates of the McKenzie mansion. Up here on Sternwood Drive, *all* the houses were mansions.

The gates to the house were open. Balloons decorated the driveway, though there was no one in sight. We walked up to the doors and they were opened, softly and efficiently, by a butler. I had never seen a butler in real life before and so I looked at him with great interest.

He was a tall, thin, balding man, in a black peaked hat and black coat and tie, and a white shirt. He looked very formal and he had large, sad eyes. He looked at us gravely.

"Yes?" he said.

Behind me, Ronny and Gordon shuffled their feet. I took out my invitation and handed it to the butler shyly. He took it from me and looked at it and nodded.

"Would the young lady care to follow me, please?" he said. "The young master is relaxing by the swimming pool."

"Yeah," Ronny said. "You go, Nelle."

"Yeah," Gordon said. "We know the way. We'll be over in a minute."

The butler ignored them. So did I. I trailed after him him into the dark cool interior of the mansion.

The butler glided along and I followed with somewhat less glide in my step. It was like he barely touched the ground. Maybe it was something you had to learn in butler school. I wondered what sort of person you had to be to become a butler.

Soft carpets covered the hallway, and on the walls hung oil paintings of elderly McKenzies, all dressed in their finest clothes (though somewhat out of fashion now) and all glaring down at me as though wondering why the butler hadn't thrown me out. I glared back at them defiantly but their stares battered me until I looked down and concentrated on following the butler's polished black shoes. The house smelled of furniture polish and pine, and the carpets were so thick you could get lost in them. Finally, after what felt like hours, we emerged out of the gloom on to the mansion's backyard. The McKenzies had a pool the size of a small country. Palm trees were arranged artfully around it and their fronds moved softly in the breeze. The pool was a warm blue colour and the water looked equally warm and inviting. Tables laden with food were lined along one edge of the grass.

There were balloons everywhere. I could smell cake and it made my mouth water.

But, weirdly, I didn't see any other guests.

Sitting alone on a lawn chair on the grass, surrounded by the buffet tables, was Waffles McKenzie. True to his name, he was eating a waffle. I stared in fascination and revulsion at the monstrosity on his plate. It was a waffle the size of a saucer, spongy and warm. On it were roasted, caramelized almonds, half-melted chocolate chips, three scoops of vanilla ice cream, two scoops of thick cream, and criss-crossing rivers of chocolate sauce that decorated it like a wobbly spider's web. On top of each scoop sat a sweet red cherry. Waffles wielded a spoon sticky with sauce. Ice cream and crumbs stuck to the corners of his mouth as the spoon moved rhythmically, empty on the way down, full on the way up. Down and up, into his mouth, which moved without stopping. His eyes had a fixed, glazed expression.

"Happy birthday, Waffles," I said.

He nibbled on an almond, then put down the spoon with a sigh. His plate was empty.

"It's Mr McKenzie to you, snoops."

I stared at him. You'd think after eating all of those sweets he'd be fat, but he wasn't. He was ordinary-looking, with a slightly too-big head that sat awkwardly on his narrow frame. It was as if everything he ate had just gone straight to his head and made it bigger and bigger, like a balloon, while the rest of him stayed the same. He wore a suit despite the heat, as though someone had dressed him, and his black hair was slicked back with gel.

"Where is everybody?" I said.

"Waffles don't share," he said. He reached for the nearest table, pulled forward a piece of cream cake and began to nibble on it delicately.

"But it's your birthday!"

"It's great, isn't it?" he said.

I looked around me again.

For a moment I felt sad for him.

"Where are your parents?" I said.

He waved his hand vaguely. "Gone. Vacation. Skiing."

"Let me guess," I said. "Waffles don't like skiing?"

For a moment his composure cracked, and I thought I saw the real him peek through from behind his eyes. "They didn't ask me," he said, so softly I wasn't sure I heard it.

"So it's just you?"

"Me and Mr Foxglove," he said. He saw my look and explained. "The butler."

"Ah."

There was a short silence and he just looked uncomfortable, like he really wanted to change the subject.

"If you were a cake," he said abruptly, "what sort of cake would you be?"

"The sort of cake that gives bad guys indigestion," I said, and he laughed.

"What do you want, Waffles?" I said.

"I don't know," he said. He put down his spoon and folded his arms in his lap. His eyes turned on me, pale and unblinking. All his attention was on me at that moment.

"You were at my boy Bobbie's place yesterday, Nelle, asking questions."

"I meant to," I said. "I didn't get very far, because someone raided his shop."

He looked pained but let it pass. "They will be dealt with."

"I don't know," I said. "I hear Sweetcakes Ratchet is on the up and up, Waffles."

"You think I can't deal with Mary Ratchet?" he said. "I've known her since she used to cry when I took her toys in the sandbox in kindergarten. Don't you worry about Sweetcakes, Nelle."

"I'm not worried," I said. "But I think you are. I think you bit off more than you can chew, Waffles. Are you just going to let her bully you?"

"No one muscles Waffles," he said, and laughed. "Anyway, *snoops*, this is nothing to do with you. Now—" He picked up his spoon again and looked speculatively at the cakes still on the tables. "Why don't you tell me why you were at Bobbie's, poking your nose in my business?"

"I'm looking for a teddy bear," I said.

"You're what?" he said, looking genuinely surprised.

"You know anything about that?"

"What would I want with a teddy bear? I'm a big boy."

"Sure you are."

"A teddy bear? You kidding me, snoops?"

He just looked bewildered, like he really had no idea what I was talking about. I figured maybe he really didn't.

"What's the deal with you and Eddie de Menthe?" I said, changing tack. "I hear you're rivals."

"Eddie?" He stared at me suspiciously. "Sure, but, like, friendly rivals, you know? I have no beef with de Menthe."

"How does that work?" I said.

"I dunno. We hang out sometimes. Ain't no crime against that, is there, snoops?"

"The name's Nelle," I said. "Or it's Ms Faulkner to you."

"Whatever you say, snoops."

I sighed.

"So you deny knowing anything about the teddy bear?"

"Get out, snoops, I don't need to steal no stinkin' teddy. I could have a room full of teddy bears of my own if I wanted. Ask anybody."

But still, he looked as trustworthy as an ice-cream seller in winter.

"You done, snoops?"

I didn't know what else I could get out of him at that moment. He could be lying or he could be telling the truth. I heard soft footsteps behind me. Turned and saw his goons shuffling behind me.

"Can we have some cake, boss?" Gordon said. His friend nudged him in the ribs nervously. Waffles's hand came crashing down on the folding table before him, sending plate and spoon and crumbs flying in all directions.

"Nobody gets *cake*!" he screamed. His face was red, his

eyes bulging. "Get out. Get *out*! All of you!" He pointed a thin finger at me. "And you! Stay out of my business! Do you under*stand* me? I won't have people interfering in my *business*! I won't have people going around asking *questions*! And I positively, definitely, *absolutely* won't have people coming over here and asking for *cake*!"

"But I didn't ask for cake," I said.

"Get *out*!"

Ronny and Gordon were backing away, slowly. I decided to follow their lead.

Waffles McKenzie was screaming and screaming, in the throes of an epic tantrum.

Then the silent butler, Mr Foxglove, appeared and whisked us away, and just like that, Waffles's birthday party was over.

9

"That was some party."

"Yeah."

"You think there'll be leftover cake?"

"Bound to be. He can't eat it all. Can he?"

"I don't know."

They looked glum as they escorted me down the hill. Behind us the gates shut noiselessly. I almost felt sorry for Waffles.

"Sweetcakes Ratchet," I said.

Gordon looked guarded. "What about her?" he said.

"She's pulling some muscle on you guys," I said.

"Yeah, well," Ronny said. "Don't you worry about the Sweetie Pies."

"Think they can take *us* on?" Gordon said. "We're not some kids in kindergarten."

"Yeah," Ronny said. "You think we got to where we are by being *soft*?"

"No," I said, "I'm sure you're real tough guys."

They glared at me. They looked about as hard as fudge.

"What about de Menthe?" I said cautiously.

"Eddie?"

"Him?"

"What about him?"

"Just making conversation," I said. A tram went past us. We were almost at the bottom of the hill and the avenue ahead was shaded with trees.

"He's all right."

"He's not a bad guy, Eddie."

"We have a treaty, don't we?" Gordon said.

"He don't poach into our territory, and we don't go into his."

"Plenty of candy for everyone."

"Sure," I said.

"Listen, snoops," Gordon said. He and Ronny faced up to me. "Boss don't want you going around asking questions. You understand?"

"Peace and quiet all round, get it?"

I looked at them. They stood there like they'd been ordered to go to the principal's office. Defiant yet worried. But doing what they were told.

"Sure," I said. I thought of the boy up on the hill, alone at his own birthday party. "Sure."

I had no intention of stopping the investigation, of course. But there was no reason to tell them that just then. Whether any of this was connected to the case I couldn't, as yet, say for sure. But a good detective asks questions first, then tries to figure out how the pieces fit together.

Then I thought about how there were two of them, and how they weren't exactly on the right side of the law, and it made me wonder, if only for a moment.

"Did you break into my office?" I said.

"What would we do that for?" Gordon said, wounded.

"Of course we didn't," Ronny said.

I stared at them hard. Could I believe them? Cody did say that the people who broke in were grown-ups. And even though he didn't really see them . . . I found it hard to believe they were Ronny and Gordon. For one thing, they were just a little too *short*.

"So we're cool?" Gordon said.

"Sure," I said.

"Good," Ronny said.

"Well, see you around, Nelle," Gordon said.

"Or not," Ronny said. "If you catch our drift."

I watched them walk back the long way up the hill.

My mind was full of unanswered questions. I had come no closer to solving the case, and I was starting to get worried. A simple missing teddy seemed to lead me directly into a brewing gang war over the illegal candy trade. Things were escalating too quickly.

I didn't even know if these events were related, but put everything together and it seemed odd. And who had trashed my office? Grown-ups, Cody told me, but he must have been wrong – grown-ups didn't go around breaking into kids' sheds and destroying what was inside – did they?

It was only a short walk from where I was up to Farnsworth Drive and, half on a whim, I turned on to it. It had been too long since I'd last been there.

Farnsworth's Chocolate Factory.

I stared at the name. It rose in wrought iron above the gates. It was so familiar that it had become just a part of the background, like the tall silent chimneys, or the walls that kept out intruders.

It was quiet here on the hill by the abandoned factory, quiet and still.

And I remembered the day the chocolate factory shut down. We all did.

The police officers, grim-faced, approaching the factory. The workers milling about in their blue overalls, some defiant but most, it seemed, resigned.

The machines were stopped.

The cocoa beans were left to rot.

The workers were made to leave.

And the chains were placed over the gates, and locked.

It was the day the smell of chocolate left the city. Like a soul departing.

They said Farnsworth never left the factory that day, that he lived there still, all alone. . .

A new police department was set up, the Bureau for Prohibition, and soon after the candy gangs were everywhere.

And no one ever saw Farnsworth again.

I began to walk around the walls. They had been topped sometime in the past with barbed wire. It sat there still, sharp and rusting. There were warning signs posted everywhere: "Do Not Enter – Danger of Death!". "Private Property – Intruders Will Be Prosecuted". "Property of the Farnsworth Candy Company, Inc. – No Unauthorized Access". There was even a sign that said, "Beware the Dog!"

While the factory could no longer make chocolate it still belonged to Farnsworth, and before he'd disappeared he'd made sure *no one* could enter his private kingdom. Perhaps he hoped to come back one day and resume production. Until then, no one was allowed in.

The walls were high and solid, with no easy foothold. Even if you could climb over and not cut yourself, you'd only be in the big courtyard in front of the factory itself.

To get to the production floor, you'd still have to get through the main doors, and those were locked and bolted.

I walked around for a long time, looking for an opening, but I found none. The wall stretched across the hill, and weeds now grew around it, and I saw ants had built a prominent nest against one corner.

On the west side of the factory, the road from out of town led up the hill to the service gates. Here the trucks used to come every morning, laden with raw materials, cocoa beans and sugar and nuts, and return in the early evening packed carefully with freshly-minted Farnsworth bars.

My mouth watered just thinking about them.

Caramel fudge with chocolate wafers so thin they melted in your mouth, tiny sugared hazelnuts that popped when you bit into them. . .

You could get still get candy, I knew that as well as

anyone. All I had to do was go down to see Bobbie, and he'd have as many chocolate bars as I could eat. A Soufflé Brothers' Special-Super-Softy-Pop, or Madame Sosotris' Three-Flava-Guava bar . . . but they'd be inferior.

No one had ever made chocolate as good as Farnsworth's.

The road to the factory appeared, at first glance, to be abandoned. Weeds grew here too, and roots broke through the asphalt. And yet when I looked more closely I saw new tyre marks on the road, and places where the plants had been crushed by the passage of something heavy like a truck.

When I went up to the side gates I saw the locks on the heavy chains had been replaced, and not long ago: they were well oiled and without the fine layer of old dust that gathered everywhere about the factory.

Could someone have been using this gate, and recently?

But if so, why?

As I rounded the boundary of the factory, the sea

came into view. The sun shone high in the sky and the blue of the water was startling.

I looked out to the horizon, and could see ships as tiny as sugar plums, and seagulls like specks of chocolate chips hovered amid the few meringue clouds. I took a deep breath of honey-scented air and, after a moment, continued to walk.

I felt I had been walking the perimeter of the factory for hours. I followed a dirt trail that had crept up into being around the walls, as though others like me had followed this same route, circling in the hope of gaining access to the mysteries of the chocolate factory.

But I could see no way in. The building kept its secrets tightly and would allow no intruders into its heart.

I reluctantly said goodbye to the chocolate factory, and went back down the hill deep in thought.

When I got home I went up to my room and sat on the bed, trying to make sense of everything in the case so far. Eddie's teddy had been stolen from the playground – that, at least, seemed clear. The question wasn't so much who the thief *was*, as anyone present in the playground at various times could have taken it. It was more a question of who, then, they were working for. Could one of Eddie's rivals – Waffles or Sweetcakes – be behind it?

So far, so simple – but that didn't explain the grown-ups who broke into my office. If they really were grown-ups, which I still found hard to believe. One way or the other, something didn't fit – and I was no closer to finding the missing teddy. There was something bigger at stake, I just *knew* it – but what?

All that was clear to me so far was that no one involved in the case wanted me to stick my nose in it. Who knew the chocolate trade was such serious business?

It was then that I thought I heard the door go, and knew my mom must have come in. I opened my bedroom door.

"Mom?"

There was no answer, though I heard someone move down below.

"Mom?"

Footsteps, but moving softly, as though trying not to be heard.

And I was suddenly scared.

I tiptoed to the stairs. I looked round for something to use, a baseball bat or a frying pan, but all I could find was a potted cactus plant. I held it up. It had thorns.

It was the best I could do.

I stepped on the stairs. The first step creaked and I froze. Down below someone moved and I shouted, "Who's there!"

There was no reply and, with a burst of panic, I ran down the stairs, my hand raised to throw the cactus. I heard an intake of breath and saw a dark, indistinct shape moving away through the open door, and then I stumbled over the carpet and the pot flew from my hand and hit the door as it closed, showering the floor with dark earth and broken shards. The door slammed shut behind the intruder and I stared stupidly at the floor, and at the cactus which lay there.

I couldn't be sure, but I thought it stared back at me with a mournful expression.

10

"Nelle? Nelle, what *happened*?"

"Mom!" I said.

My mother stepped through the door and looked aghast at the mess.

"Are you all *right*?" she said.

"Oh, Mom," I said. I didn't burst out crying, but I felt close. She helped me up and held me to her. I pressed my face against her, feeling her warmth and smelling her perfume and sweat. "I love you, Mom."

"I love you too, bunnyhug," she said, and I smiled.

She used to call me that when I was a baby, but now she only used it when I needed a cuddle.

"Did you see anyone run out of the house just now?" I said.

"No," she said. "Did anyone. . .?" She held me at arm's length and looked into my face. "Are you. . .?"

"I'm fine," I said.

"Oh, Nelle!" She hugged me again, pressing me close to her. "We'd better call the police," she said.

"Wait." Something had caught my eye. I pointed. "What's that? Did you bring it home?"

My mom looked puzzled. "I have no idea what you're talking about, sweetheart."

Sitting by the door was a small, square box. It was the sort of box you used to carry hats in. It was tied with a black ribbon.

I had a bad feeling about the box.

"It's not mine," I said softly. My mom was reaching for the phone when I said, "Wait," again. I went to the box and prodded it gingerly. Nothing moved inside. It could still be full of snakes, I thought, or a poisonous spider, or a bear trap.

"A bear trap?" my mother said. "What *are* you talking about, Nelle?"

"Sorry," I said. I must have spoken out loud. I peeled back the black ribbon and opened the box cautiously.

Then stared at what was inside.

"That's strange," my mother said.

Inside the box was an old teddy bear.

I took it out and held it up to the light. He was a beat-up old teddy with brown fur that'd been washed so many times it looked dirty grey. He was missing his left eye and there was a patched hole in his chest that looked like a bullet wound that'd been sewn shut. He was missing a part of his right ear. He had a cute, black button nose.

And he had an original label, too faded to read, but I knew that, if I could only read it, it would say, "Farnsworth".

It was Eddie de Menthe's missing teddy bear.

"Someone broke in," my mother said, "to deliver a teddy bear? Nelle, what is going on? Are you involved in anything I should know about?"

"I don't know, Mom," I said honestly. I turned the teddy in my hands. He looked old and cuddly. "His name's Teddy," I said.

"That's original."

"I'd better put him away," I said.

"Nelle. . ."

"It's fine, Mom. Really. It's just . . . a case I've been working."

"You're not a private detective, Nelle! No one is! Only people in cheap paperbacks, or in the movies!"

She sounded so worried, but it still hurt when she said it.

She could see my reaction, and her face softened. "I'm sorry, sweetheart. But this isn't a game, this is serious. Someone broke into our house! I'm going to call the police."

"I understand." I gave her another hug quickly, then took the teddy without saying anything else. I took him to my room and put him on the bed next to Del Bear. She sulked for a moment but didn't say anything.

"Look after Teddy for me," I said.

I went back to the living room. My mom had tidied up the broken pot and replanted the cactus. They were hardy things, cacti. Like private detectives, they took any amount of beatings and still went on. My mom had changed into her house clothes and now sat on the sofa with the television on. She looked tired, but she smiled when she saw me.

I was going to tell her about my investigation, and Waffles, and the playground, and marbles and candy and missing teddy bears and Sweetcakes Ratchet and the chocolate factory, and perhaps I started telling her, and my mom said, "Slow down, Nelle, I can't understand a word you're saying," when there was a knock on the door.

"It must be the cops," my mom said. She looked relieved. I followed her to the door and she opened it.

There were two of them, a man and a woman. The man was thickset and balding on top, unshaved, with a shirt one size too small for him. He wore a bad suit and a bad haircut and what looked like a permanent scowl.

The woman was his opposite. She wore a crisp linen suit and an expensively-cut bob and dark mirror

WELCOME

shades despite the hour. She was tall and thin and she smiled the way a shark does when it sees you swimming towards it like a happy meal.

"I'm so glad you're here," my mom said. "I only just called about the break-in."

The two of them exchanged glances.

"What break-in?" the man said.

"Was anything stolen?" the woman said.

"No, no, I don't think so," my mother said.

The woman just shrugged. "Then this isn't our problem," she said, and my mom bristled.

"Then who are you?" she said. "And what do you want?"

"I'm Detective Tidbeck," the woman said. "Ma'am. And this is Webber. May we come in?"

Tidbeck made to follow through but my mom didn't budge. "What is it about?" she said.

Webber came to life, as though he were a mechanical doll switched on, with groaning limbs, at the press of a button. His voice was the sound of a car engine stalling.

"Missing Persons," he said. "We're looking for

one – ” he made a pretence of studying a small notebook he brought out of the breast pocket of his suit – “Edward, AKA Eddie, de Menthe. Age twelve and a half. He’s gone missing.”

“He lives with his grandmother on Falcon Drive, but she hasn’t seen him in three days,” Tidbeck said. “She’s very concerned.”

There was as much warmth in her voice as a winter storm. She made me think of snow flurries and being out alone without a coat.

“Eddie?” my mother said. “What happened to Eddie?”

“We don’t know, ma’am.”

“That poor boy,” she said. “Did you hear that, Nelle? You remember Eddie, don’t you? You used to play together when you were little.”

“I don’t remember,” I mumbled. My voice was very small. Both detectives turned their heads as one and registered me.

“You’re –” again, Webber consulted the notebook – “Nelle?”

“Yes.”

"We were told the de Menthe boy came to see you –" another glance at the notebook – "two days ago? Around noon?"

"Who told you that?"

They ignored the question. Tidbeck pushed up her mirrored sunglasses. Her eyes were cold blue marbles underneath. "Did he, Nelle?"

My mom turned to look at me, concern written on her face. "Did he, Nelle?" she said quietly.

"Yes," I said. "It was just. . ."

"What did he want?"

"It was nothing," I said. "Really."

"I heard you like to play detective," Tidbeck said unexpectedly. Webber laughed. It was the sound of rocks avalanching. His whole belly shook.

Tidbeck smiled, with what apparently passed for human warmth. It was like watching a store mannequin stretching its mouth.

"You *do*?" she said. "That's so *sweet*!"

"Do you have a *licence*?" Webber said. His belly continued to shake. I stood there, red-faced and angry.

"Please do not make fun of my daughter," my mom said, and I could have hugged her at that moment. She stared stony-faced at the detectives.

"Nelle," she said, "did Eddie come to see you?"

"Yes," I said. There was no room to avoid the question, not when she was like this.

"What did he want?"

"He was just looking for something," I said. "Something he lost."

It didn't feel like it was a big deal to tell them the truth, and yet there was something about the detectives I really didn't like, and it made me hesitate.

Tidbeck and Webber dropped their smiles. They dropped them as though they'd never worn them, as though they had been masks all along.

I could see hunger in their eyes and it made me afraid.

"What was it, Nelle?" Detective Tidbeck said. "What was Eddie de Menthe looking for?"

"Answer them, Nelle," my mom said. All this time her eyes were on Tidbeck and Webber.

"His teddy bear," I said. I saw no reason not to tell them.

"*His* teddy bear?" Detective Webber said.

"His *teddy* bear," Detective Tidbeck said.

My mom looked surprised. She began to smile, then stopped when she saw how serious the two detectives were. They were both staring at me like I was a bar of slowly-melting chocolate.

"And did you *find* it, Nelle?"

"Did he tell you where it *was*, Nelle?"

"What is this really about?" my mother demanded. "Why are you so interested in a teddy bear? And why are you questioning my daughter?"

"This is very important," Detective Webber said. "What did he tell you, Nelle?"

"Nothing," I said. "He told me nothing. Is he really missing? What happened to him?"

Webber and Tidbeck exchanged glances. Tidbeck slipped the mirrored shades back over her eyes. I could see myself reflected in them like a fly.

"That is what we are trying to establish ... Miss Faulkner. Here. My card," Tidbeck said. She passed it to me. It had her name on it, and a telephone number. "You call me if you hear anything. We're all *very* concerned about poor Eddie."

"Think of his grandmother," Webber said. "How she worries."

"Day or night," Tidbeck said. "You'll let us know?"

"Sure," I said. I slipped her card into my pocket. "But I don't know where he is."

"You take care now," Webber said. "Ma'am. Little girl."

"It's Nelle," I said. "My name is Nelle."

His eyes narrowed, just a little. "I'll be sure to remember that," he said. "Tidbeck?"

"Let's go," she said. She nodded to us and executed a turn and they both walked off without a backwards glance. I stared after them.

They got into their black car and drove away.

11

In the morning I woke abruptly. One moment I was deeply asleep. The next I was wide awake. I lay on my back and stared at the ceiling. Morning light played on the walls. I couldn't help thinking about the case, and I wondered what I'd let myself in for. I realized that I'd seen the detectives' car twice before, and it meant that either they were following me, or they were somehow wrapped up in Eddie and Waffles's chocolate business. Why else did they keep showing up?

And what exactly did it all *mean*?

It felt safe in the bed. Safe, and warm. I didn't want to get up. I didn't want to face the outside world. Beyond my bedroom the world wasn't nice and it wasn't comfortable, and if I left my room I didn't know what I would end up finding.

Eddie was in trouble, I knew that. And there was no one to help him.

But he'd come to me for help.

I *had* to help him.

And that meant I had to *find* him.

I had only one clue. The missing teddy bear.

The same missing teddy bear that was currently perched at the end of my bed.

After the two detectives left the night before, I'd had a hard time explaining to my mom what was going on, because I wasn't totally sure myself. Finally I went to my room and then I picked up the worn-out old teddy and looked at it closely.

I wondered if maybe there would be a clue inside it, but when I pressed its tummy and felt round its head, I couldn't feel anything other than soft squishy stuffing.

I didn't want to cut it open. It looked like it had been through enough already.

"Farnsworth", the faded old label had once read.

Why Farnsworth? How was *he* tied into this?

It wasn't a dead end, it was something, but I didn't yet know *what* it was.

I stared at the ceiling. I smelled French toast cooking. It was comfortable and warm and safe in bed: but you can't stay in bed for ever.

So I got up and I got dressed and I brushed my teeth and I went downstairs and had breakfast with my mom. I drank half a cup of milk. Then I kissed her goodbye and did what every good detective should when they don't have any leads: I went to the library.

It was another hot day, hot enough to melt chocolate, if only you could buy any. On my way I passed the playground on Malloy Road. Despite the relatively early hour the sentries were already standing guard on the door in the fence, and I saw a trickle of kids heading that way with their hard-earned pocket money.

Across the road under the shade of the trees I

saw a now-familiar black car. I went the long way around so they wouldn't see me, but I knew Tidbeck and Webber were there. They must have been watching the playground, hoping Eddie would turn up. Who were they, really? Why were they looking for Eddie, and why were they asking questions about the teddy bear? Were they even really from the police?

Further on my way, on Mandarin Road, was a call box. I went inside and phoned the police line.

"Can I speak to Detective Tidbeck at Missing Persons?" I said.

"Hold on, please." I was put on hold and a moment later the phone rang again and a woman's voice answered, "Detective Bureau."

"Oh, hello," I said. "I was looking for Detective Tidbeck at Missing Persons."

"Tidbeck? You must have made a mistake, Tidbeck's with the Bureau of Prohibition, they report directly to the mayor's office."

"She's with *Prohibition*?" I said.

The voice sighed. "Yeah, the Banned Candy

Bureau," she said, in what definitely sounded like a sort of disapproving tone.

"And her partner? Webber?"

The voice on the other end of the line was still. "Who is this?" she said.

"I'd rather not say."

"Are you in some kind of trouble, kid?"

"I don't know," I said honestly.

"I don't mean to tell you your business," the voice said, "but it would probably be better if you stayed away from those two."

"That might be too late."

"My name's Levene," the voice said. "Detective Suzie Levene. If you need to talk, call me. Or tell me where you are, and I'll—"

"I have to go," I said. "Thank you." And I hung up. I stared at the receiver. After a moment the phone rang and made me jump. I hesitated, then picked it up.

"Hello?"

"This is Levene. Listen, kid, I want to help—"

I hung up again. This time I didn't stick around. I left the phone booth and heard the phone ring again, the sound growing fainter as I walked at a quick pace up the road. I'd been right not to trust Tidbeck and Webber. But how did I know Detective Levene was any better? I couldn't trust anyone – anyone grown-up. I was on my own. . .

And Tidbeck and Webber were obviously mixed up in all of this – I thought suddenly of the two shadows Cody had described to me, the ones he saw break into my office. It was a thought that I'd had at the back of my mind ever since last night, and a thought I'd tried hard to push away – only it kept coming back.

Grown-ups, Cody had said. And I thought of Tidbeck and Webber sneaking into the backyard and smashing everything in my office, in total silence, looking for – what?

The teddy.

I felt suddenly very cold, despite the warmth of the day.

12

The library was a pleasant single-storey building with a white stone facade and ivy growing over the walls. I climbed the short steps and went in.

It was a clean well-lighted place and I went past the children's books shelves and mysteries to the back, where the research centre was. It was darker and quieter there, mostly deserted but for a couple of older people placidly reading the morning papers.

I went up to the librarian and she helped me find what I needed.

It is a useful rule of the professional detective: when in doubt, ask the librarian.

I began looking for the Farnsworths in the Local Interest section, where the librarian had directed me. Among books on home-grown movie stars, unsolved murders, haunted mansions, dairy production, local geography and pirates, there was a section set aside for the chocolate factory and for the Farnsworths themselves. I took an armful of books and went to a seat by the window, with my back to the wall, and began to read.

There was surprisingly little information I could find. The Farnsworths had lived in the city for three generations, beginning with old General Farnsworth who, having retired from the military, first established the Farnsworth Candy Company, Inc. The business grew modestly at first. The general's son expanded the business but died in an unfortunate chocolate-related accident just five short years after the birth of his own boy.

The book had a photograph from the funeral. All the dignitaries of the day were there: the mayor, two film stars and an Oscar-nominated director, the ambassadors of Brazil, Peru and the Ivory Coast, an exiled princess of Romania with a black veil over her face, a former vice president, the owner of the local baseball team, the conductor of the national philharmonic orchestra, two generals, three major industrialists, a world-renowned playwright, and a minor member of the British royal family in a very expensive-looking coat and hat.

The heads of the other chocolate companies were also there – Madame Sosotris, The Soufflé Brothers, Benny Bonbon, Edmonton St Creme-Egge and Borscht.

They posed together for the camera, with the hard looks of people who didn't really want to be there. It was the first time I had seen them, and I studied the old photograph with interest.

Madame Sosotris was a tall, thin woman with a big wide hat, and big yellow teeth like a horse's. The Soufflés were short and fat: one was bald and one had a thick head of black hair like liquorice. Borscht just scowled – he looked like a grumpy maths teacher – and

Benny Bonbon looked bored. Edmonton St Creme-Egge was dressed in a black suit with a top hat and white gloves over long fingers.

The boy – the present Farnsworth – stood with his back to the camera. Now he would be a grown man, but he was only a boy then. He wore a sombre dark suit tailor-made to his smaller size. He was holding his mother's hand. This was the widow Farnsworth who had taken over the family business and with an iron fist expanded it into a worldwide empire.

But the boy. His fine hair was slicked back against his scalp. His hand gripped his mother's tightly as the coffin was lowered. It was a black and white picture and the sky was grey, the ground dusty, the assembled dignitaries frozen for ever in the photo. They towered over him.

I felt so sad for him then. I knew how he'd felt.

He was so small, and so alone.

But not entirely. I looked closer and, of course, it was there. With one hand he was holding on to his mother. With the other he held on to a friend. He hadn't yet lost his eye, and a part of his ear, and his coat of fur was shiny and new, but I knew him all the same: it was Teddy.

I stared at the young boy and his teddy bear, and then I turned the page quickly. How had Eddie come to own Farnsworth's old teddy, and why were people looking for it now, all these years later? I wanted – *needed* – to know!

The rest of the book was irritatingly vague. The young Farnsworth grew up. He went to college. He enlisted in the air force, was wounded in battle, received a commendation and was honourably discharged. He took over the Farnsworth Candy Company after his mother's death, and seemed to have taken to the job with ferocious enthusiasm. The company's influence grew even further, and Farnsworth chocolate bars and Farnsworth sweets and Farnsworth candy were sold everywhere from Chicago to Timbuktu. The factory became the single largest employer in the city.

And that, pretty much, was that.

I decided to look through the newspaper archives next. The librarian helped me with the microfilm machine and I flicked through the old scanned pages.

Though the factory and the Farnsworth Candy Company were often mentioned, I could find no more photos of Farnsworth himself. He seemed to have gone to a great deal of effort to ensure no photos of him were ever taken.

Then, when Thornton became mayor and the factory was shut down, Farnsworth just disappeared. No one knew where he went, what he did.

He had lost the one thing that was most important to him, his life's work: the chocolate factory.

It was so unfair!

But it did not get me any closer to finding out where Eddie de Menthe was, or why Tidbeck and Webber were after him, or why the teddy bear I'd been hired to find was now hiding in my bedroom.

I rubbed my eyes. They were sore and I needed air.

On my way out, I saw the librarian behind her desk. When she thought no one was looking, she opened her drawer and quickly drew out a chunk of chocolate and put it in her mouth. When she caught me looking she shut the drawer quickly and pretended to fill in an index card.

I pushed through the doors and out – and ran smack into Sweetcakes Ratchet.

13

"Watch where you're going, *Nelle*."

"This the gumshoe?"

She had two of her girls behind her, Daisy and Rosie, and they circled around me, one on either side, and began to push me playfully between them.

"Stop it," I said, angry.

"Stop it!" Daisy imitated me, laughing.

"*Stop* it!"

"Make me!" she said.

"Oh, look, she's going to *cry*," Rosie said. Sweetcakes watched them with a tolerant smile. They kept shoving me between them like I was their new favourite plaything.

"What are you doing here, Nelle?" Sweetcakes said.

"I was returning a book," I said. "This *is* a library, Mary."

"Are you being smart again, Nelle? This is *my* patch. Did Waffles send you? Are you spying on me?"

"Why would Waffles send me?"

"Maybe he wants his candy back!" she said, and barked a laugh.

"Whatever's between you is none of my business," I said.

"Unless you work for him now," she said, and snarled. "Heard you went up to his place."

"That's none of *your* business, Sweetcakes."

"But that's where you're wrong, Nelle. Candy *is* my business!"

The next time I was shoved I pretended to stumble. Then I came up low against Rosie's legs and *pushed* hard, and she stumbled and fell.

I was already in motion, jumping after her and over her body as she lay there crying.

"Stay out of my library, Nelle!" I heard Sweetcakes scream behind me furiously. "Stay out of my territory, or I'll get you!"

I was running, running so fast my heart was trying to escape through my ribcage and my throat hurt and all I could hear was the beating of blood in my ears. I finally slowed down when I was sure no one was following me.

So Sweetcakes was selling candy out of the public library, I thought. I was angry, and a little horrified at the realization.

It made sense. It was a perfect location.

Kids came in and out of the library all day long and no one paid them any attention. It was the perfect excuse to say, "Mom, I'm going to the library!" and then, in a quiet corner of the reading room, meet a Sweetie Pie and get something sweet.

Contraband candy, I thought. It was *every*where.

But now I knew for certain the old teddy bear *was* Farnsworth's, I had another avenue to try. I had the beginnings of a plan.

I went back home to get my bike. It still needed

fixing after the beating it got from the Sweetie Pies outside Bobbie's place.

I popped back into the house and made lunch. In my room, I saw the teddy looking at me with his single glass eye. He seemed very lonely and sad, as though he missed his owner. I put him into my school bag gently and closed it. He would be snug and warm there. There was a place I could take him where I might get some answers, but first I needed to fix my bike. I ate quickly, took my bag with the teddy in it, and then I wheeled the bike back on to the mean streets.

I avoided the playground and the library. The bike repair shop sat on the beginning of the slope at the start of Lennox Avenue. The breeze from the bay brought with it a refreshing coolness, a tang of salt. It was hot pushing the bike up the hill, and the straps of the bag pressed into my shoulders. I was relieved to find shelter at the shaded entrance to the bike shop.

A bell chimed as I walked in. The interior of the shop smelled pleasantly of glue and oil. Miss Redfearn, the bike mechanic, was sitting on a stool in her grease-stained overalls, tightening the screws on a pedal.

"Hello, Miss Redfearn."

"Nelle. I'll only be a moment."

I watched her work. She was quiet, intent on the job at hand. There was a look of concentration on her face. Her black curly hair stuck to her forehead with the heat and she pushed it away. Finally she was done. She settled back with a satisfied look. When she turned to me, her full concentration followed with her.

"How's your mom? How can I help you today?"

"She's fine," I said. And, "It's my bike, it's. . ."

"Let me see." She got up and wiped her hands on a rug and came over and took the bike from me. She looked it over, concern written on her face.

"This poor thing!" she said. "Who did this to her?"

"Just some girls," I said.

"They won't be welcome in *my* shop," she said. She stroked the front wheel lovingly. "We'll take care of you, don't worry," she said to the bike.

"Will it take long?" I said.

"A couple of days, probably," Miss Redfearn said. She used to teach gym class at school and she was always nice, but you could tell she liked bicycles more than children. I guess they made more sense to her than we ever did.

I said, "Miss Redfearn, I need it really fast."

"Why is that, Nelle?"

Sometimes, she still sounded just like a teacher.

"It's for a job. I can't really explain. Please?"

"You mean an *investigation*?"

I shrugged, a little uncomfortably. Grown-ups always thought I was play-acting, that a girl couldn't really be a detective. But they were wrong. And I was going to prove it to them, by finding Eddie.

But a soft smile momentarily lit Miss Redfearn's face. "I always wanted to be a detective..." she said.

"Did you?" I said, surprised.

"When I was a girl," she said. "Then I grew up..."

I watched her. Her hand spun the bent wheel of my bike. "All right," she said. "Let me see what I can do."

"Thank you," I said. I watched her carry the bike over to her workspace, where she set it down carefully. The radio was on and the last notes of a song faded and an announcer said, "And now for a word from the mayor."

"Thank you, Bob. Hello, I'm Mayor Thornton."

Even on the radio, he sounded like he was smiling, with all those even white teeth. "Three years ago, you elected me to represent you. Together, we have made this city better, stronger, and healthier! But there is more, so much more to be done. We must work to bring back our glorious city, to tear down the old and bring in the new! I say to you now, we must tear down only to *build!* New roads, new houses, new—"

"No, no, I just wanted music," Miss Redfearn said. She turned the dial on the radio until she found something classical, then nodded in appreciation and went back to looking at my bike.

"Miss Redfearn?"

"Yes, Nelle?"

"You know Mr Thornton?"

"The mayor?"

"Yes."

Miss Redfearn pinched the tyre on the front wheel and looked at it sadly. "I've never met him," she said, "if that's what you mean."

"Oh."

"But I voted for him."

"You did?"

That took me by surprise. She heard it in my voice and smiled. "Yes," she said. "As it happens, I agreed with him."

"You're a Prohibitionist?"

She shrugged. "You shouldn't eat sweets, really," she said. "They're bad for you. Riding a bike is healthier."

"But what about choice?" I said. "I thought. . ."

"You know," Miss Redfearn said, "not *everything* is about candy, Nelle. Thornton's not a terrible mayor. The city's done no worse under him than under most other mayors."

"But it's not *fair!*" I said. "You can't just tell us what to *do*!"

"Well, we *can*," Miss Redfearn said. "I mean, you're *kids*. This is how the system *works*. No, there is no need for you to make that face, Nelle."

Miss Redfearn frowned in concentration as she dismantled my bike.

"When you get older, Nelle," Miss Redfearn said, "you'll see not everything in life is fair."

Then she stopped and shook her head and smiled a little sadly. "No," she said. "I hope you never do."

"I know things aren't always fair," I said quietly. I thought of my dad. I thought of Eddie, lost or hiding somewhere. I thought of the smell of chocolate that used to be everywhere in the air and now wasn't. "But they ought to be."

Miss Redfearn was frowning at the bike. Her hands moved dextrously as she worked.

"I know," she said at last, and shook her head. "I used to feel that way too."

Then she said, "Come back in an hour, Nelle. I'll have the bike ready for you by then."

Outside, the sun was bright and the traffic was in full flow, cars passing both ways, a dog barking, a police siren wailing urgently in the distance. Life wasn't fair, I knew that, but it *ought* to be. I still believed that, and I knew I always would.

Three doors down from the bike repair shop stood my real destination: Mr Lloyd-Williams's Trinkets, Teddies & Toys Emporium. My dad had bought me Del Bear there, when I was a toddler. Teddies, party hats, cowboy and witches' costumes hung in the windows, and I went in.

The interior was gloomy and crammed with aisles. I loved coming here. I could spend hours rooting through the disordered toys and trinkets, and now I spent a pleasurable moment looking at a vial of fake blood, a whoopee cushion, two plastic toy pistols, a camera that shot out water when you pressed the button, a box of multi-coloured marbles and, finally, a cowboy hat.

I put on the hat and looked at myself in the mirror. "Think you're tough, do you?" I said. "What was that? Are you talking to me? I don't see anybody else here, are you—"

"Talking to me?" a voice said irritably, and I jumped. "Are you talking to me? I can't see you, child."

I removed the cowboy hat and hung it back on its hook, and went through a cramped aisle to the counter, where old Mr Lloyd-Williams stood glaring at me. He was tall and stooped, with white hair and a white moustache, and a crisp English accent like a bad actor in a horror film. He and the shop had been there for years.

He wore a cream double-breasted suit despite the

C
A
B

heat, and a red plastic flower in the lapel that shot water in your face if you tried to smell it.

Everyone knew never to shake hands with him, because he always wore a shock hand buzzer for just such an occasion. They said he used to be a real clown, in an actual circus, I mean.

"Oh, it's *you*," he said.

This was his standard greeting, so I didn't take offence.

"Hello, Mr Lloyd-Williams," I said politely. I'd never met anyone else with a hyphenated surname.

"Nelle," he said. "Nelle . . . Franklin."

"Faulkner," I said.

"Yes, yes," he said irritably. "I knew that. How is Delphina?"

He never remembered our names properly but he knew each and every teddy bear he'd ever sold. That was why I'd come to see him.

"She's well, thank you," I said.

"Good, good. You look after her, you hear me?"

"I will. I am."

"Good. Well, would you like to buy something, child?"

I could see he'd already forgotten my name again. The store was empty. I thought he must have been napping until I had come in.

"It's quiet," I said, for something to say.

He grunted. "Quiet month," he said. "Quiet year. Might have to close down the shop."

"No!" I said, in genuine horror. I couldn't imagine the shop not being there. My dad had always taken me. He'd bought me my first detective kit there.

Mr Lloyd-Williams nodded. "Yes, yes," he said. He had very white and very bushy eyebrows and they moved up and down as he spoke, like the hands of a conductor in front of a full orchestra.

"No one ever comes to see me any more," he complained. "They say I only sell old junk and the shop smells of cat. I don't even have a cat."

"Cats are nice," I said.

"Horrible creatures!" Mr Lloyd-Williams said with a shudder. "They have new shops now, in the big malls, big shops with all the same toys in them. Aisles and aisles and not an exploding cigarette to be seen. They never come here. Your father used to come here, you know," he said abruptly. "With *his* father. That's loyalty. That's *tradition*. And then when he grew up and had you, he brought you to see me. I never forget a kind word or a bear's face, but people still forgot me. Now I sit here for hours, dreaming, but nobody comes anymore. Perhaps I'll go back to England, though it's a dismal place, cold and it's always raining. I don't like the rain. Do *you* like the rain, child?"

"I . . . don't mind it?" I said, wondering how to get him back on track, and he harrumphed, and said, "Well, it's a terrible thing, rain, and bad for my bones, you know."

"I didn't."

"When you get to my age. . ." He peered at me. "How old are you?"

"Twelve."

"Twelve! I must have been twelve once, but I genuinely don't remember. I'm seventy-eight, you know."

"I didn't know that."

"I should be retired!" he sighed, and looked quite pleased with himself. "They all came here, back in the day," he said. "There wasn't anyone who didn't pass through my shop. The president came once! The president! Unfortunately there wasn't enough time for a picture."

"Everyone?" I said. This was what I was counting on.

"I knew them all. The movers and the shakers, the high rollers and the lowlifes." He shrugged. "Everyone needs a toy or a teddy or a trinket, sometimes," he said.

"Mr Lloyd-Williams?"

"Yes, child?"

I took the teddy bear out of my bag and held it up for him. "Have you ever seen this teddy before?"

"A bear? You come to me with a bear?"

"Please."

"Wait a minute." He rooted under the counter and returned with a pair of curious-looking glasses, with a magnifying glass attachment over the left eye. He donned the glasses and picked up the teddy bear and looked at it closely.

"Ah. . ." he said. He turned the teddy over gently, pressed its tummy, looked behind the one remaining ear. "The poor thing," he said. "Yes, yes. A custom job. I remember it now."

"You do?"

"I know every teddy bear I ever sold," he said. "I remember this one like it was yesterday. It was for the Farnsworth boy."

Finally, I thought. I tried not to show my excitement. Mr Lloyd-Williams needed to be coaxed gently, before he forgot the topic again and wandered off.

"Tell me about him," I said.

"The Farnsworth boy. I knew his grandfather, the general. Very stern man, the general. Didn't approve of toys. Didn't approve of chocolate much either. Liked the money he made off it well enough, though. Grew orchids. Why orchids, I don't know. Awful things. Smell funny. Went up to the house once, you see. Saw him at the greenhouse. Servants everywhere and all that rot."

He looked at me blankly. "What was I saying?"

"The boy," I prompted, trying and not quite managing to stay patient.

"The boy. . ." Mr Lloyd-Williams's eyes softened. "His daddy brought him to me. *He* never had toys.

The general didn't approve. But this was his boy, and he was going to do things his way. A good man. Tragic fate. Fell into a vat of boiling chocolate. Fell, or was pushed, no one could say. But, anyway. He came to me with the boy. Never seen anyone so excited. The boy, I mean. It was like he wanted to try *everything* in stock. Whoopee cushion. Thought it was the funniest thing he ever saw. Costumes! He tried them all on. Cowboy, pirate, astronaut, ballerina. Water pistols! Loved them. It was like he'd never been to a toy store before."

"Maybe he hadn't," I said.

Mr Lloyd-Williams nodded. "I suspect you're right," he said. "And all the while the father stood where you're standing now – though, of course, he was taller than you are now – he stood on the other side of my counter and watched his boy play, and he smiled. That was all. He didn't say anything, and the smile was just that, a smile. But it was in his eyes, and it stayed there the whole time his boy was playing. Then, finally, he turned to me and he said, 'Mr Lloyd-Williams, I would like to buy my son a teddy bear.'"

I looked at the teddy on the counter between us.

He was old and grey and wounded: he'd been through the washing machine of life and come out through the cycles, sometimes up and sometimes down, but still here. He'd been loved and cherished.

"You see the label?" Mr Lloyd-Williams said. He stretched it between his fingers, examining it with the magnifying glass. "Farnsworth," he said. "I sewed it on myself. In a way, this teddy is more of a Farnsworth than anyone else still alive."

"Anyone but the boy," I said, and for a moment he looked startled.

"The boy, yes. Of course. But he is hardly a boy any more."

We were silent for a moment, watching the faithful old companion. I had so many unanswered questions. What had made Farnsworth part with it? How had it come into Eddie's hands? And why were Tidbeck and Webber looking for it?

"Is it valuable?" I said. "Does it have some great value, or . . . is there anything hidden inside, something that, I don't know . . . a key or a map or. . .?"

Mr Lloyd-Williams picked the teddy up and

examined it carefully. Finally, he shook his head and laid the bear down again gently. "I don't think it's been tampered with," he said. "It is possible, I suppose, but I doubt it. It is just an ordinary teddy."

"But it must be valuable," I said. "It's so old and . . . and it's a Farnsworth!"

He picked the bear up and passed it to me. "It's just an old, ordinary bear," he said. "Listen, child. You're asking the wrong question. Of *course* it's valuable. It's priceless. But only to the person to whom it belongs."

I stared at him, wordless.

Inadvertently, Mr Lloyd-Williams had handed me a piece of the puzzle.

The teddy bear on his own had no value. But it meant something to its owner.

That was why they were after it.

They weren't after the teddy bear itself. They were after its *owner.*

They were trying to find Mr Farnsworth.

15

When I got home, a note had been slipped under the door for me. It said:

> *Be outside the shop at eight o'clock tonight if you want to learn more. Tell no one. Do not approach.*
>
> *Bobbie*

I stared at the note, wondering what it meant, feeling apprehensive about going, knowing that I would all the same.

Things were going sour in the candy trade, and I

wanted – needed – to know why. Eddie was missing, Waffles was panicking, and Sweetcakes Ratchet was on the war path.

It was enough to give anyone stomach ache.

That evening I waited until my mom thought I was fast asleep and snuck out of the house while she was watching TV. I left the teddy safely at home. I wheeled the bike until I was clear and then rode it the rest of the way to Bobbie Singh's place. My bike looked almost new. The front of Mr Singh's shop looked the same as ever

At eight o'clock sharp a big silver car pulled to a stop in front of the shop and a man with sad mournful eyes and a butler's uniform stepped out of the driver side. He opened the passenger door and out came Waffles McKenzie.

He stood still for a moment chewing his lower lip thoughtfully, as though he'd never seen such a dump before and wasn't sure he ever wanted to again. Then he nodded to himself, said something to the butler, whose name, I remembered, was Foxglove, and went in.

He wasn't inside for more than five minutes and when he came out again Bobbie Singh was with him. They spoke briefly before Foxglove opened the car door and Waffles slid in and they were gone. I watched Bobbie stand there watching them drive off into the distance. He didn't look happy but then, he seldom did any more.

I waited as Bobbie went back inside. Then he left and got on his own bike and cycled away and I followed.

We rode through quiet streets where the street lamps winked alive as the sun set and night settled on the city. The air was warm and scented with flowers. It made me think of when I was young, last summer, before I was a private eye, and Bobbie and I played together and rode our bikes with nothing more to do than have fun. Now I followed him, unseen, as he drove to the meeting point. It was just beyond the point the city ended and the rest of the world began.

There was a gas station on the road that led out of the city. The factory towered overhead on the hill. The sea was nearby, and I could smell the salt and beach fires and hear distant laughter and gulls' cries coming from the direction of the beach.

Bobbie parked his bike in the deserted car park, then stood beside it and waited.

I watched from across the road.

A truck came along the road, driving towards the city. It slowed and turned at the last minute, then entered the gas station and parked in the car park. The engine stilled. Bobbie watched. The driver came out and whistled. Bobbie ambled over. I saw them speak briefly. Bobbie gestured angrily. The driver shrugged. Bobbie looked at his watch, pointed. The driver shrugged again. Bobbie looked from side to side. Nodded. He followed the driver to the back of the truck and the driver opened the cargo bay and—

The sound of a police siren shattered the night. It rose and fell like waves breaking, like nails against glass, like a baby who wouldn't stop crying. It demanded attention. It filled everything until it was the only sound left in the world. I covered my ears. The siren swept past me and with it came the flashing blue light, and a familiar black car.

It roared across the asphalt and into the car park and came to a stop with a screeching of brakes, blocking escape. Bobbie and the driver stood, frozen. The car doors opened in unison and slammed in unison and two familiar figures emerged into the night under the pale yellow light of the street lamp.

It was Tidbeck and Webber.

"Well, if it isn't little Bobbie Singh," Tidbeck said. Her voice carried. The light caught her pale, sculpted face and the amused cruelty in her eyes. "Isn't it a bit late for you to be out on your own, Bobbie?"

Bobbie just stood there.

"What's in the truck, partner?" Webber said. The driver shrugged sullenly. Webber's steps across the concrete were like the beats of a drum. He peered inside the truck and whistled.

"*Chocolate*," he said, loathing in his voice. Tidbeck grabbed Bobbie's ear between her fingers. He didn't make a sound, though his face twisted in pain. Tidbeck dragged him with her and looked inside the truck.

"You know anything about this, Bobbie?" she said.

"You could feed the city for a month on this junk!" Webber said. The driver spat on the pavement.

Webber turned to him. "Who do you work for?" he said, in quiet menace.

The driver shook his head. "I ain't telling you nothing," he said.

Webber smiled grimly.

"Who's behind this shipment?" he screamed. "The Soufflé Brothers? Madame Sosotris? Edmonton St Creme-Egge? Is it Borscht?"

"Is it Borscht what?"

"Wrong!" Webber said, and his heavy fist rose, but Tidbeck grabbed his arm.

"I ain't doing nothing wrong!" the driver yelled, shocked out of his seeming boredom. "Ain't illegal to carry candy!"

"It is across the city line," Tidbeck said. "And this *is* the city line."

I saw Bobbie rub his ear and steal a glance at his bike; but he knew there was no getting away. I was afraid for him, afraid for myself. I could feel the blood beating in my ears. Should I run away?

But I couldn't leave Bobbie behind.

"More importantly," Tidbeck said, with quiet menace, "this is a chocolate shipment *we* didn't authorize. *We* don't get our *share*. Now why *is* that, do you think? So I'll ask you again, who *authorized* this . . . this *un*authorized shipment?"

"I don't know nothing!" the driver said. "Besides, I ain't across the line."

I stood very still where I was. So Tidbeck and Webber were a *part* of the chocolate smuggling operation? They were *profiting* from it!

The driver glared at them sullenly. "You folk in the city are crazy."

"Crazy or not, the law's the law," Tidbeck said.

"Yeah," Webber said. He smiled unpleasantly.

"It's just candy!" the driver said. I could sympathize.

"Rots your teeth," Tidbeck said.

"Rots your gut," Webber said.

"So you go back to the Consortium," Tidbeck said. "You go back to your bosses, those *chocolatiers*."

Chocolatiers. That meant chocolate makers, I knew.

But she'd said the word with awful contempt.

"You go back and you tell those vanilla-bellied candy pushers, this is *my* town! You tell them to *stick* to the *arrangement*. Oh, and the price of doing business has just gone up. You *tell* them—"

"I'm just a driver!" the driver said.

"You tell them –" Webber yelled, waving his finger in the driver's face. I saw Bobbie try to make himself as small as possible.

"– that the price of doing business is now thirty-five per cent," Tidbeck said.

"Thirty-five!" the driver said, shocked.

"Yes," Tidbeck said.

The driver shrugged. "I'll tell them," he said. "But they won't like it."

"They don't have to like it, buddy," Webber said. "All they gotta do is pay up."

The driver shrugged again. "And the stuff?" he said. "Do I take it back, or what?"

"Who said anything about taking it back?" Webber put his arm around the driver's shoulders. His smile had the sticky quality of fudge. "Come on," he said. "I'll buy you a coffee."

He led the other man towards the station. Tidbeck was left alone with Bobbie Singh. She smiled at him. She looked like she'd only ever practised it in front of the mirror.

"I hear Eddie de Menthe's gone missing," she said conversationally. Bobbie stared down at his feet. The wind carried their voices to me as clear as if I were standing beside them.

"I guess," he said.

"Know where he went?"

"Don't know nothing," Bobbie said.

"Anything," Tidbeck said. "I don't know anything."

"That's what I meant to say."

Tidbeck sighed. "Bobbie, I'm not the bad guy here," she said. "I'm just trying to help you out. I know you're in a bad spot. Eddie's on the loose, Waffles is too busy eating the merchandise rather than selling it, and that little girl, Sweetcakes, she's not that sweet, really, is she."

It wasn't a question and, involuntarily, Bobbie shuddered.

"I don't know nothing," Bobbie muttered sullenly. He did a pretty good impression of the truck driver.

"Listen to me, you little—" Tidbeck said, and then she stopped and tried on a smile again, but it didn't take so she dropped it. "Listen, Bobbie. We let you kids play. Why not? You all get what you want – as much candy as you can eat, the Consortium get to sell their candy inside the city, we provide security and get our cut of the proceeds, and everyone's happy. Right?"

"Right," Bobbie said.

"What we *can't* have is any more *shenanigans*. And more importantly, what we *really* can't have is a lack of *stability*. Not right now. Something's going down, Bobbie, and I think you know what it is."

"I don't—"

"Know nothing. Right." She pinched the bridge of her nose. "I want Eddie," she said. "I want Eddie, and I want what he knows. You get back to your boss and you tell him, little Bobbie Singh. Or I could take you with me right now and book you into juvie."

Juvenile Detention. Bobbie looked up at her in horror and I froze in place. "You wouldn't," he said.

"Try me."

"I don't know where Eddie is!" He was going

to spill and she knew it. "I don't . . . he came to see Waffles. They were friends! He saw him all the time, up in the house. He had this crazy idea that if only he could find Farnsworth, if only he could make him come back from wherever he went, he could make everything better again. He said we needed to go back to being just kids. He was tired of running a gang. He said he'd found something, something important, that it could lead us to Farnsworth."

Tidbeck was very still. When she spoke her voice was soft and low; but it carried. "What was it?" she said.

"I don't know!" Bobbie was close to tears. "It was just a story, something he made up. Waffles didn't care. He just liked having him around. Waffles doesn't really have any friends."

"But you have a friend, don't you, Bobbie?" Tidbeck said. "That little girl. What is her name? Nelly? Little Nelle?"

I felt as though someone had dumped cold ice cream all down my back. Bobbie blinked up at Tidbeck.

"Nelle?" he said nervously. "What about her?"

"She's been snooping around," Tidbeck said. Her voice was low and menacing. "Asking questions. Sticking her nose where it doesn't belong. What does she know, Bobbie?"

"Nothing!"

"What does she *know*?"

"I don't know!"

"Then make sure you find out," Tidbeck said savagely. She poked Bobbie in the chest with her index finger and he staggered back. Tidbeck exposed white sharp teeth. As though it had been a signal, her partner stepped out of the café and came to join her.

They stood together and conferred in low voices. Webber laughed. He looked at Bobbie and gestured at the open truck.

"Well, get on with it," he said.

"Sir?"

"You got a job to do, don't you? Then do it," Webber said. He and Tidbeck went back to their car and climbed in and a moment later they drove past me, back towards the city.

Bobbie stared after them with big haunted eyes.

16

I ran to Bobbie.

"Nelle!"

"Bobbie, are you all right?"

"I'm fine," he said. "Honest."

I looked at him, both worried and relieved that it was over. The note said I would learn more if I came, and I did – far more than I'd bargained for. I tried to make sense of it all in my head – the discovery of Tidbeck and Webber's role in the candy trade, the fact that they *must* have been the people who broke into my office too – the whole involvement of *grown-ups* in what only a few days ago seemed to me to be just a game.

It was a lot to try and make sense of.

"What is going on, Bobbie?" I said. I grabbed him by his shirt. His small sad face looked up at me mutely. "What do you *know* about what's going on?"

"You heard what I said! I know what Eddie was looking for. *Who* he was looking for. But not just that. He figured he was close. No one knows what Farnsworth looks like. He could be anyone. They say he changed his name and disappeared. Just like that." He snapped his fingers. "Eddie said it's all gone on too long. The Consortium of Chocolatiers are behind it, Nelle. The Soufflé Brothers, Madame Sosotris, Edmonton St Creme-Egge and the rest. Borscht."

"Borscht?" I said. Bobbie shrugged.

"They were the ones who pushed Farnsworth out. They hated him, Nelle. He was the best. Do you remember?"

I thought of rich creamy chocolate and sour strips and crunchy bars, and my mouth filled with saliva. "I remember. . ." I said softly.

"They helped Thornton get elected and they made candy illegal and they put Farnsworth out of business. But Eddie said he could change it. He was tired. He didn't want to be a bootlegger any more."

"But how do you *know* all this, Bobbie? If this is true it's. . ." I didn't know what to say. "Huge."

"You'd have to talk to Waffles about that," Bobbie said. "I just sell the candy, Nelle. I never asked for the rest of it. Or to get involved with those two detectives. They scare me."

"They scare me too," I said.

But something still didn't seem right. I had more of the puzzle pieces, but I felt I was still missing a few. The Consortium seemed too distant. Could they *really* be behind it all? Behind Prohibition?

But Prohibition started when the mayor came into power. So what did that mean? Did the Consortium *help* Mayor Thornton? Or did they just use the opportunity that was created for them when the mayor came into power and passed Prohibition?

The truth was, I just didn't know.

"Why are you telling me this now, Bobbie?" I said.

"Eddie said if he were ever in trouble then he'd come to you," Bobbie said.

"Me? Why me?"

"He liked you. He said you used to play in the sandbox together when you were small. And he said you were good. You weren't involved like we are."

"I am now," I said.

He lowered his head. "Yes," he said. And, "I'm sorry."

"You don't have anything to apologize for, Bobbie."

When he looked up at me his eyes were very bright. "Are we still friends?" he said.

"Of course we are."

"I'm worried, Nelle."

I patted his shoulder awkwardly. "I know."

"I never asked to be dragged into this. At first it was just a way to make some pocket money. It was just a bit of fun. You know? Then my mom got sick and my dad was worried about the bills and now I never leave the store unless it's to do . . . this." His hand swept over the abandoned car park, the truck, the streetlamp that cast us in a yellow pool of light.

"I don't remember the last time I played a game, Nelle," he said.

I didn't know what to say to him. He was my friend and he was lost.

"It will be all right, Bobbie," I said gently. "I promise."

"If you say so, Nelle."

"I do," I said – with more conviction than I felt. Then, "Hey, Bobbie, what happens to all this candy?"

I looked at the parked truck. Bobbie didn't say anything.

Instead, he stuck two fingers in his mouth and whistled.

The whistle cut through the night like a butter knife. It rang through the clear air, a piercing, high cry.

For a moment, nothing happened. There was no one around for miles, or so I thought.

Then the night exploded with motion.

They came from everywhere, at once. They came out of the shadows, and I realized with shock that they had been there all along.

I had thought – like Tidbeck and Webber no doubt had – that we were alone.

But we weren't.

They came on their bicycles, from every street and road that drained on to the highway. From the hill and from around it, from all directions: kids on bicycles, Bobbie's boys, Waffles's gang. They were the candy couriers, the sweet smugglers, the chocolate runners.

They swarmed over the truck. It was all done in efficient silence. Boxes were carried out of the truck and passed from hand to hand. Then the first bike departed, a young girl cycling furiously, a box of candy on the back seat of her bike. Then another, a boy this time, and then another, and another, shooting out of the car park, across the highway, and into the city.

They all took different routes, as one by one they disappeared into the night.

They streaked like candyfloss ghosts across the horizon, the only sound that of wheels spinning on asphalt, and by the time the truck driver emerged from the abandoned café of the filling station, a cup in his hands, the truck was empty, and Bobbie and I were the only ones left.

Silence lay over the sleeping world. The tail-lights of a passing car illuminated the curve in the road and passed into the night.

Even the gulls had stopped their crying.

On the hill above us the chocolate factory squatted, immense and dark and closed. It was a place of magic and mystery, unknowable and unknown.

And a thought came unbidden into my mind, and wouldn't go away, as unlikely as it first seemed.

"What if Eddie's there?" I whispered. I looked sideways at Bobbie. "What if he's hiding in the chocolate factory?"

Bobbie looked up at the moonlit factory on the hill. His eyes were bright and round.

"Why would he do that?" he said.

I said, "It's the only place they wouldn't dare to look."

17

I followed Bobbie as we rode our bikes across the road and back into town. We cycled in silence.

The night rose all around us as we cycled. Night has its own special silence. Ahead of us the couriers had pedalled fast with their cargo of illicit candy.

Then I saw light on the horizon, as though it were dawn.

But sunrise wasn't due for hours.

The sky changed colour as licks of yellow and red streaked the air, and I began to smell smoke.

I stole a glance at Bobbie. His face was pale and his

eyes were fixed dead ahead. He pedalled faster and I tried to keep pace.

As we cycled towards his street, the smoke rose higher in the sky and I could see the flames.

"Dad!"

Bobbie's voice came out as a strangled cry. His skinny legs went up and down, up and down on the pedals, until I thought the bike itself might catch fire. I couldn't match him. He rode the bike like his life depended on it, and he left me behind.

When I turned the corner I saw the store was in flames.

"Dad! Dad!"

The shop window of Mr Singh's store had been smashed, and flames billowed out, sending heavy smoke into the street. It rose into the air and the flames competed with each other in which could reach higher.

I heard a fire engine siren in the distance, anxious and wailing, coming closer.

"Dad!"

Bobbie braked the bike and began to run, the bike falling behind him. The door to the shop opened and Mr Singh staggered out. His turban was missing and his hair fell down his face and shoulders in a dark shower.

"Dad!"

I ran after Bobbie as he tried to lead his father away. The heat was intense and I felt my eyebrows and hair scorch. I took one of Mr Singh's arms and Bobbie took the other and together we pulled him away from the burning building.

The siren grew louder and louder and a fire truck appeared. Fire fighters streamed out and hands were pulling us away to safety. Someone pushed a bottle of water into my hands and then I was drinking and the world was cool and dark again.

"Is there anyone still inside?" a fire fighter said.

Mr Singh stared at his shop. He shook his head. "No," he said. "No, there's no one, I just. . ." He shook his head again helplessly. "I got out, but then, I thought I could save . . . I went back, I thought I could. . ." His voice died. He stared at his burning shop.

The fire fighters set up their pump and began to shoot jets of water at the building, which roared back at them as the fire tried to escape.

There was nothing I could say. I sat with Bobbie and his dad, watching their shop go up in flames. I thought of all the little treasures on the shelves and how someone had once made them and now they were gone. And I thought of the little room at the back, and all the chocolate bars in their wrappers, all melting away to nothing.

"What happened?" Bobbie whispered.

Mr Singh shook his head. It seemed all he was able to do.

"Was it an accident?"

But we both knew it wasn't, even before Mr Singh shook his head again wordlessly.

"Sweetcakes," Bobbie said quietly, out of his father's hearing, and there was hatred in his voice.

"You don't know that!" I said.

But Bobbie had spotted something I didn't. He kneeled down and picked up a familiar red-and-pink polka dot bandana.

It was the exact same one I saw Sweetcakes wearing during the stink bomb attack.

"She wanted the business," Bobbie said. "She wants to take over the candy racket, take over Waffles's turf, and Eddie's. This was a message. And all the candy!" He sounded desperate. "Waffles is going to kill me."

"Sweetcakes is just a kid!" I said. "She's a kid like us. She wouldn't set the place on fire. This is something else, something different. I don't care if you found some bandana. It doesn't prove anything. Maybe that she was here, but that's all, Bobbie! She probably dropped it the last time she was here. I mean, this wasn't a stink bomb. People could have been hurt!"

"You think people weren't hurt? Look at it! It's gone! It's all gone!"

"Bobbie. . ."

"What, Nelle? *What*?"

I didn't know what to say. The fire fighters had managed to control the blaze. The fire was fighting back but it was losing, shrinking. It had nowhere to escape and it was starved of oxygen now. I saw lights flashing and heard a siren approach, and a car I recognized well by now pulled in beside us.

Doors opened and slammed shut, and Tidbeck and Webber sauntered over and stood beside us, watching the dying flames.

"Nasty," Tidbeck said.

Webber munched on a health bar. Chunks of oats fell from his mouth as he chewed. "Hope you're insured," he mumbled.

I saw Bobbie shoot his dad a glance. Mr Singh nodded and I saw Bobbie's shoulders relax.

The fire was dying. The smell in the air was awful, like wet burned hair and cat poop and sick. Webber ambled over to the captain of the fire fighters and stood talking to him in a low voice. Tidbeck remained by us, her eyes on the ruined shop.

"Such a shame," she said.

There was no compassion in her voice, and I shivered. She turned, as though she could read my mind, and smiled.

"Nelle, Nelle, Nelle," she said. "You seem to turn up everywhere, don't you?"

I dug my nails into the palm of my hand and didn't answer, and her smile widened.

"Just *everywhere*," she said thoughtfully.

I watched her eyes. She had the eyes of a toad. They were eyes that fixed on you and never blinked, and tracked your every move as though you were a fly she wanted to eat.

Her hand landed on my shoulder, lightly. The fire hissed as it finally went out and the shop was left a wet ruined stump of a building. Tidbeck turned to Mr Singh and Bobbie. "Take care now," she said.

She didn't say anything else. She and Webber disappeared into their car and drove off. The captain of the fire fighters came over to talk to Mr Singh, and Bobbie gave me a sad little smile and didn't say anything; there was nothing really to say.

When I came up to the house my mom burst out of the door, gave a strange little cry and held me tight.

"Where have you been, Nelle?" she kept saying. "Where have you been?"

"I went to see Bobbie," I said. "I'm sorry I snuck out."

She sniffed me through her tears. "You smell of smoke!" she said.

"There was a fire."

"I know there was a fire! Nelle, what did you get yourself *into*?"

"I was riding my bike with Bobbie, that's all!" I said. It wasn't a lie. It just wasn't all of the truth. "When we came back his place was on fire."

"What happened? Do they know what happened?"

"It was a fire," I said inanely.

"Oh, *Nelle*," my mom said. She released me and stood there looking at me with heavy eyes. "I think someone broke into the house again when you were gone. I heard a noise and when I got up to see what it was, I found out you were missing."

"Someone broke in?" I had a sudden bad feeling.

"Well, I don't know for sure. If they did then they didn't take anything. Nelle, what's going on? Are you involved in something dangerous?"

"We were just playing. . ." I said, but unconvincingly. My mom took me by the hand and into the house and shut the door on the world. All the anger seemed to drain out of her and she just looked tired, and happy that I was there. I could see she had questions, that there were all kinds of things that she wanted to say, but then she saw the look in my eyes and just stroked my face instead.

"Come on," she said. "I'll make you a warm milk."

While she was busy in the kitchen I went to my room. I knew what I would find – or rather, what I wouldn't – even before I went in.

I looked everywhere, but finally I had to admit defeat.

The teddy bear was gone.

18

In the morning, Waffles McKenzie came to see me. I'd gone to the shop for milk and when I came back I saw his big silver car was parked on the street outside, and his man, with the same sad mournful eyes and a butler's uniform, stood beside it, waiting patiently.

"Mr Foxglove?" I said.

His eyes brightened up momentarily, and he nodded and took off his peaked black hat. "Miss Faulkner," he said gravely. "It is good to see you again."

"And you," I said. If it was hot for him inside

the uniform he didn't show it. I wondered again how he'd come to be a butler but it didn't feel appropriate to ask.

"The young master is awaiting you in your office," he said.

"Then I better go and see what he wants," I said.

He put his hat back on and nodded. "Goodbye, Miss Faulkner."

"Goodbye, Mr Foxglove."

I went into the garden to find Waffles. He was standing there looking at my house chewing his lower lip, like someone who'd turned on the TV only to find a cartoon they didn't very much like. Then he saw me and his face brightened, and he said, "Ah, Nelle. I was just looking for you."

"Have you been waiting a while?"

He waved his hand airily, but I could see that his hair stuck to his forehead with sweat.

"Come in," I said, taking pity on him.

He followed me into my office and then stood there chewing on his lip some more and looking around him with the same mournful expression.

I took a seat behind my desk and gave him his time. I wasn't in a hurry to go anywhere.

"This your office, then?" he said finally. As a conversation starter it was a no-go but I let him have it. He looked at my bookshelf but I don't think he even saw it.

"Uh-huh."

"It's kinda small, ain't it?"

"It has a desk and it has chairs, and do you want to sit down, Mr McKenzie?"

"You can call me Waffles," he said absent-mindedly, and sat down. I looked at him across the desk, thinking this was the second time this week one of the major bootleggers in this town had sat there, and that the last one had gone missing shortly after.

"How can I help you, Waffles?"

He took out a packet of chocolate buttons and popped it open and chewed morosely on a handful. He saw me looking and offered me the pack. "You want some?"

I waved the offer away. He looked quiet, and a little sad, and I thought of the last time I saw him, alone on his birthday: not even his parents came.

"That fire last night," he said.

"Yes."

"You were there."

"Yes."

"People could have been hurt, Nelle!" he said. "People *were* hurt."

"I know."

"All my cargo is gone," he said. He munched on a few more buttons. They left sticky trails of melted chocolate in his palm. "Now I'll owe the Consortium even more, and those detectives from Prohibition."

"Tell me about it, Waffles," I said, but gently. I could see that he wanted to talk. I had to keep myself from pushing him too hard.

"What's to say, snoops?"

"Tell me how it all came about."

"Take longer than a month full of sundaes," he said. But then he shrugged.

"It all started about six months after Thornton was elected, and Prohibition came into effect," he said. "To start with, it was just casual smuggling. You know, people go out of the city, to visit relatives, or on holiday or for a day out, and when they come back they bring candy with them. Kids go along with their mom and dad on trips, and come back having spent all their pocket money. Then some of them realize they can't eat all the candy by themselves, and they start selling it to their friends at school."

"Sure," I said. "That makes sense."

"You can see where this is going. Some kids have easy access to the candy. Their mom or dad work in another town or they have regular visits to grandma in Bay City – but maybe what they *don't* have is ready cash. So eventually little gangs start forming. Candy clubs. Someone has to fork out the cash for the candy, so that someone else can buy it outside the city, bring it back and then sell it on, for a cut. Before too long the gangs start fighting with each other as the trade grows. The Raisin Gang, the Kandy Krew, the Chocaholics, they're all fighting for control, each rising from their own school or neighbourhood, trying to take over the city."

"Sure," I said. "But how do you come into it?"

"I was just a small fish, snoops. But I had big

dreams. See, when all this was going on, *I* was trying to take over, but I was running into problems. For one thing, as I'm sure you know, there was a new police department, the Bureau of Prohibition, and they started to block the candy coming into the city. Suddenly, all my couriers were stopped at the city line. Candy was getting confiscated, parents were being told they'd get fines if they were caught bringing anything in. Maybe worse. In short, snoops – I was having a problem."

I leaned forward, interested. "So what did you do next?"

"That's a good question."

"So?"

"I didn't do nothing, snoops. But one day I got a phone call. You know . . . be at this place at such and such a time on such and such a date. And my dad, well, he wasn't around much at the time on account of his work and all, but my chauffeur took me to Bay City, where you know candy is *everywhere*—"

"Where it's Christmas every day, and it rains cola, and chocolate grows on trees?"

"Exactly. And maybe, just maybe, I was a little bit nervous because I didn't know who it was on the phone, only that she sounded a little scary, but just maybe I kind of had a guess. . ."

"That your luck was about to change?"

"Right. So I get to the place and the woman on the phone turns out to be Madame Sosotris, of Sosotris Sweets and Snacks, Inc."

"You don't say. . ."

"And with her are the Soufflé Brothers and Edmonton St Creme-Egge, and Borscht, and finally, Benny Bonbon, of Bonbon and Bonbon Bespoke."

"The tailor-made confectioners?"

"The same."

"The five families. . ." I said.

"Only now they've all joined forces," he said. "And they call themselves—"

"The Consortium?"

"Yes."

"But that's *grown-ups*," I said. "That's not just bringing it in for other kids. That's *serious* stuff, Waffles."

"Yeah, well," he said. "I know these people. My folks are rich too."

I couldn't argue with that.

"So what happened?"

"They made me an offer," he said quietly. He looked away from me.

I said, "It was an offer you couldn't refuse?"

"Uh-huh."

"But you didn't *want* to refuse it, did you, Waffles?"

"They offered me candy, Nelle. All the chocolate I could ever eat! All the sweets I could ever sell. All the ice cream in the world. And free waffles!"

"And all your supply problems gone, just like that."

"Ah, but they weren't, were they?" Waffles said, and the half-smile he gave me was half-sad. "Because I still had to get the candy into the city. And there was still the Bureau of Prohibition. . ."

"So about that," I said.

"I came back to the city and soon enough, everything they said came to be. The trucks started coming, stopping right outside the city line. The Consortium wasn't – isn't – strictly speaking, breaking the law. They don't bring the candy into the city themselves. That's down to me – and I have enough kids working for me to make the contents of a truck disappear in a couple of minutes."

"I know," I said. "I saw it for myself."

"You've been busy, snoops."

"It's what I do," I said.

"Do you want me to go on, or not?" he said testily.

"Please, no, do go on," I said.

"Thank you. So, the trucks start coming, my ... *empire* keeps expanding, and those two cops from Prohibition, Tidbeck and Webber? Turns out they can be quite ... *accommodating.* They and the Consortium have a deal, I guess. So Tidbeck and Webber make sure everything's going smoothly and get a cut of the proceeds. And, I mean, it's not like there's anyone to stop them. After all, No one *really* cares. It's just kids. It's only candy. And it's a stupid law anyway."

"It might be stupid," I said. "But it's still the law."

"Whatever."

"So the other gangs can't compete with you, and

they either get broken up or they're made to . . . join in. Right?"

"That's right, snoops."

"But not *everyone's* gone," I said softly. "Are they, Waffles?"

"No," he said. He looked uncomfortable.

"Not Eddie," I said.

"No. . ."

"But *why*, Waffles? If the Consortium is working exclusively with you – then *where does Eddie get his candy from*?"

Waffles smiled wide, but without humour, and shrugged.

"Now *that*," he said, "is a very good question."

learn something," he said cryptically.

It made me think about the mayor. I tried to put the facts of the case together in my head. Far as I could make out, the Consortium were behind it all. *They* had pushed for Prohibition. *They* profited from it, now that candy was illegal. *They* were behind the mayor.

Or were they? Tidbeck and Webber had made it clear they had some sort of arrangement with the

ene that

ice. But did

ment? Or was he

health of the city's

part of it too? Did the

all the way up to the top?

elieve it.

atter what I wanted to believe. What

o was find out more. I decided to start by

ack to the library, where I knew I would find

etcakes.

Bobbie was convinced that Mary Ratchet had set the fire, but, whichever way I thought about it, it just didn't add up. It was true that Sweetcakes was a bully, but could she really have set fire to Mr Singh's store? Something about it didn't feel right to me and I was determined to find out more.

I decided to walk to the library. I didn't want my bike trashed again by the Sweetie Pies. It was a nice morning, not yet too hot to be outside, and for some reason, even with everything that had been going on, I felt good. I even whistled as I walked along

Altman, enjoying the shade of the old wide trees and the quiet.

Too quiet. I was almost at the library when they jumped me from behind the trees.

The Sweetie Pies.

Daisy and Rosie, and Little May.

"What do you want!" I said.

They surrounded me in a half-circle. There were three of them and only one of me, and whenever I tried to move away they blocked me off. They were grinning, like sharks anticipating blood pudding.

My heart was beating fast and my palms were sweating. I backed away and felt hands on my back, and heard Rosie laugh as she pushed me. Daisy grinned and pushed me too and the two of them began to shove me back and forth between them, while Little May jumped up and down as though she'd eaten too many sweets.

"Told you . . . to . . . stay out of our *way*!" Daisy said.

"You got to leave alone, Nelle!" Rosie said. She sounded almost frustrated.

"I want to talk to Sweetcakes," I said.

"Well, you can't! She don't want to see you!"

"You can't stop me from going to the library," I said.

"Told you to stay off . . . our turf!"

"Stop sticking your nose in other people's business!" Daisy said.

"That's right! That's right!" May shouted.

"Did you burn the shop?" I said. Being pushed around wasn't so bad, really. At least that's what I was trying to tell myself.

"Now why . . . would we do . . . that?" Daisy said.

"You want to . . . take over. . ." I was breathing hard by now and had to keep stopping to take in air. "The candy . . . trade."

"You think we can't take on two little boys?" Daisy sneered. "Waffles and de Menthe, put them together and it just sounds . . . *disgusting*!" And with that she pushed me, hard, and Rosie stepped aside, laughing, and with no one to catch me I fell, and rolled on the ground, where all I could see were the dainty little shoes on Little May's feet, going up and down, up and down.

Then, laughing, they sauntered away, back towards the library.

I stood up slowly and dusted myself clean.

"This isn't over!" I shouted after them. My heart was still going fast and I wasn't whistling any more. But I wasn't hurt, and I was fine. If you set off to shake a beehive you should expect to get a few stings along the way, and not just honey. It wasn't nice, but it was what happened when you were a detective. It may have started off as just a game, but growing up was serious business – and so was candy.

20

A black car passed slowly down Altman. It made me wonder how long it'd been there. It rolled slowly, as though its driver had all the time in the world.

I watched it grimly until it had rolled its way towards me and stopped. I expected the by-now familiar faces of Tidbeck and Webber, but when the window came down I had a surprise.

The driver looked out and smiled.

"Nelle Faulkner, I presume?" she said.

Her voice sounded familiar but I wasn't sure for a

moment where from. She had brown hair and a nice smile and a cop's voice.

"We talked on the phone," she said. "I have to admit you're a hard person to track down."

"You're that detective," I said, realizing. Remembering when I'd called the Detective Bureau and got—

"Suzie Levene," she said.

"How did you find me? I didn't give you my name."

"I'm a detective, I find people."

"Fair enough," I said, and she smiled. She looked like she smiled easily.

"What do you want, Detective Levene?" I said. If I'd been in a good mood before then it had evaporated like the steam that comes off hot milk.

"Can we talk?" she said.

"What about?"

"You called the station," she said. "I wondered why."

"Wrong number?" I said, and she laughed.

"Try again," she said.

"Look, Detective Levene—"

"You can call me Suzie."

"*Detective* Levene," I said. "I can take care of myself."

"I want to know why you called the station asking for Detective Tidbeck," she said, and she was no longer smiling.

"Why?"

"You know, Nelle," she said, and pinched the bridge of her nose as though she had a headache coming on, "we're not all like Tidbeck and Webber."

"You enforce Prohibition," I said.

"Prohibition's the law."

"But it's not *fair*!" I said.

"Life isn't always fair!" she said. I glared at her.

"Look, Nelle, there's a difference between enforcing the law because it's the law, and profiting from it. After your call, I did some digging, and I didn't like what I found. I could use your help on this."

"What do you care?" I said. "It's just chocolate, isn't it? Isn't *that* what you think?"

"Sure," she said. "And if it *was* just chocolate, maybe . . . I guess that's how they got away with it for so long. I mean, who would care, right? So maybe it's my fault too, Nelle. For looking away, or not looking at all. And you know what, sure, I can let all that go because it's all just *kids*, right? I can let all that go and look the other way because it's just *candy* and I have real crimes to deal with and real criminals to catch?"

"Right," I said.

"And then a kid goes missing and a shop goes up in flames, and suddenly I can no longer look away, Nelle. Suddenly, this has become a part of my *job*."

"That's an impressive speech," I said, "but what's any of it got to do with me?"

She sighed. It was quiet in the street and I didn't see anyone else about, but it didn't mean to say there wasn't anyone watching.

"I want to help you, Nelle," she said. "And maybe you can help me too."

"How?" I said.

"Tell me what you know about Tidbeck and Webber. What they've been doing."

"I don't know nothing," I said.

"I don't know *anything*," she said, correcting me,

and sighing again. "You think you're so tough, don't you, Nelle?"

"No," I said. And I didn't. I just didn't trust her, even though I wanted to.

Maybe she could see it in my eyes.

"I'm not going to say you remind me of myself at your age," she said. "Although you do, a little . . . look, Nelle, I just want to help. Your friend, Eddie, he's missing. Don't you want to find him?"

Were Eddie and I friends? It was a question I wasn't sure I could answer. But I did want to find him.

"He could be in real trouble," Suzie Levene said. "And with Webber and Tidbeck after him . . . well, I wouldn't want to be in your friend's shoes, Nelle."

"All right," I said. I took a deep breath. "Maybe we can help each other. But there's something I need you to look into for me first."

"What?" she said.

"I need to find out about Mr Farnsworth," I said.

"The man from the chocolate factory?" she said.

"Yes."

"You think he's connected to all this?"

"I don't know for sure, but I think he might be," I said grimly. "I was hoping to find out."

"I did look him up, as it happens," Detective Levene said. "Out of curiosity. But there was nothing to find. He has no file, no driver's licence, no bank account, no home. For all intents and purposes, he doesn't even exist."

"But he does," I said.

"He must do, somewhere. Just not on file."

"Is that possible?"

She laughed, without much humour. "It shouldn't be, but it is."

"Don't you think that's odd?" I said.

She gave me a long look. "Yes," she said. "Yes, I do. But he's not committed any crime that I know of."

"What about the other *chocolatiers*?" I said. "Do you know anything about them? The ones from Bay City?"

She shrugged. "Not really. Again, I did some digging. I know Madame Sosotris was born in Detroit, that the Soufflé Brothers are not actually brothers but cousins, that Edmonton St Creme-Egge lists his hobbies in the *Who's Who* as 'gardening, classical music and collecting antique harpoons', and that Borscht is a kind of beetroot soup. At least, I think it is."

"Beetroot soup?" I said.

"Maybe," she said dubiously.

"So you have nothing?" I said.

"I'm a cop, kid, not a miracle worker," she said. "What about you? What can you tell me?"

I wondered how much I could trust her.

In truth, I wasn't sure that I could, but I also didn't have any other options. I had to trust someone. And Suzie Levene seemed honest, and she said all the right things. I took a deep breath, counted to ten in my head, and decided to take a chance.

I told her what Waffles had told me. When I had finished, she looked troubled.

"I think you should leave the rest of this to me," she said.

"And what are you going to do?" I said.

"I don't know. But I do know you should stay out of it."

"Are you warning me off the case?"

"This isn't a *case* you can solve, Nelle! This isn't a game. When you grow up you can apply to join the police force, and if you're accepted you could go through the academy, and train to become a police officer, and *then*, if you work hard and pass the right tests, eventually, you might become a *detective*."

"Like you," I said.

"Exactly. Yes."

"Like Tidbeck and Webber?"

She was silent. Then, "Every barrel has a couple of rotten apples."

"Even with all the *training*, and the *tests*?" I said.

"That's not what I meant."

"I might be twelve, Detective Levene, but it doesn't mean I like to be treated like a child."

She was silent again, and then, after a moment, she laughed, a little in embarrassment. "Fair enough," she said. "I'm sorry."

"It's all right," I said. "And if it helps, I promise to try not to get into trouble."

"That's quite a promise," she said, still with a little laughter in her voice.

Then: "So where will you go now?"

I thought it best to avoid the library, for the moment. But there were other avenues to pursue.

"I thought I'd visit Eddie's grandmother," I said.

"Well, at least *that* seems harmless," Detective Levene said, with some relief.

21

Falcon Drive was a long narrow street with box-like apartment blocks on either side of it. In a children's playground a little girl rode a tyre swing back and forth, and two little boys fought a pretend duel with sticks. I could feel eyes in the windows, behind curtains that twitched but never opened. In the distance I heard a police siren, which was abruptly cut off. It was quiet here, and yet it was an alert sort of silence. The sound of my footsteps felt very loud to me, and I was relieved when I reached the building's entrance. The buildings were old and rundown, and I saw a large sign hung up on the wall. It said the block was soon to be renovated by Thornton Construction. I'd seen the picture on it before, outside the playground on Malloy Road. It showed Mayor Thornton smiling as he perched on a crane, wearing a bright yellow hard hat.

I pressed the buzzer and waited. There was no reply so I pressed it again, longer this time, until I heard a handset being lifted and dropped and then lifted and an irate voice say, "What? Who is this?"

"Mrs de Menthe? My name's Nelle, and I'm here about your grandson?"

I heard her breathing into the handset. "Who sent you?" she said.

"No one," I said, startled.

"What did you say your name was?"

"Nelle. Nelle Faulkner."

I heard her breathing some more as she deliberated. I shifted my weight from foot to foot, wishing I could get off the street.

"Come on up," she said at last, and I heard a harsh electrical buzzer sound. I pushed the door open and went inside.

It was dark on the stairwell and smelled of boiled cabbage. It was carpeted but the carpet was dirty and worn. I climbed up carefully until I reached the third floor and knocked on the door.

"Yes, yes, I'm coming," the irritated voice said. I heard her moving inside the apartment and then she opened the door. She was old and stooped, with curlers in her blue-white hair, and big chocolate-brown eyes that looked at me suspiciously from behind thick glasses.

"What do you want?"

"I was hoping to . . . can I come in?"

"What was your name again?"

"Nelle Faulkner!" I said, shouting a little.

"Don't raise your voice to me, girl," she said. "Faulkner, Faulkner." Then her eyes grew softer and I realized she wasn't angry or confused – she was just very worried.

She held the door open and I stepped inside. Unlike the outside, the apartment was comfortable and bright. The furniture looked old but was clean, and there was the smell of something good cooking in the oven.

I followed her into the living room. Photographs covered the walls. They were mostly of Eddie, Eddie as a baby, Eddie as a young boy holding his father's hand, playing on the swings, Eddie barefoot on the beach, feet in the sand, laughing, Eddie with his grandmother on a cliff somewhere with dragon-like clouds curling in the background, Eddie with. . .

"You are his friend?"

I stared at the picture. She saw me and smiled. "I remember you now," she said. "You used to play together when you were small."

"So I keep hearing. But I don't remember."

"Pictures don't lie," she said, with satisfaction.

In the picture, Eddie was playing in the sandbox with a small, serious-looking girl.

The girl was me.

"He always spoke fondly of you, you know," Mrs de Menthe said. "Your dad and his dad worked in the factory together back in the day."

The factory. That's what we all called it. We never had to say *which* factory. For us, for everyone in the city, there was only ever one.

I stared at the picture. Eddie looked happy. So did I. We must have been three or four years old. Mrs de Menthe disappeared into the kitchen and I could hear her bustling around. I looked at the picture again. Was that really why he'd come to me? I felt guilty and wasn't sure why. He'd trusted me. I didn't want to let him down.

"Do you know where he is?"

"Excuse me, dear?" She reappeared in the living room with a tray in her hands. "Can you help me with the drinks?" she said.

I took the tray from her and placed it carefully on the low table. Her hands were shaking, though she tried to hide it.

"Please, please," she said. "Drink."

I stared at the table.

On the tray were two hot chocolates and a plate of cocoa wafers. The hot chocolate was topped with whipped cream and crowned with partially melted marshmallows. It was the sort of drink that, even if it weren't already illegal, should have been a crime. Clearly, Mrs de Menthe didn't play by the rules. Perhaps that explained her grandson's attitude.

I took a sip. It was like drowning in sugar.

"Do you know where he is? Eddie?"

Mrs de Menthe shook her head. "He'll be fine," she said – but she sounded like she was just trying to convince herself.

I took another sip and bit off a marshmallow. I couldn't help it. It was delicious.

"Eddie was living with you?" I said.

"There is no one else," she said sadly.

I buried my nose in the hot chocolate. I didn't know what to say.

"Have the police been around?" I said at last.

She made a dismissive gesture. "Two cops with bad manners and worse suits," she said. "They keep asking questions and poking their noses in but I don't think they wish anything good on my grandson."

"A man and a woman?" I said.

"Yes."

"Webber and Tidbeck," I said. "They were asking questions at my house too."

"He's too smart for them," Mrs de Menthe said. But I could see it was hope more than faith in her eyes. She was scared. She was worried for Eddie.

And I was too.

I picked up one of the cocoa wafers and put it in my mouth.

The taste was one I had almost forgotten, though you never forget a Farnsworth chocolate biscuit, not really.

It reminded me of the open factory gates, of my dad emerging with the other workers, smiling when he saw me, and opening his arms; of a happy sun shining down on a world infused with the smell of fresh chocolate. Of days that seemed to last for ever, and there was no cloud in sight to darken the sun.

"Where did you *get* this?" I said, when I could speak again. Mrs de Menthe looked at me without comprehension.

"The cocoa wafers? From the kitchen."

"Can I look?"

I didn't wait for her reply. I jumped to my feet and went and peered around into the kitchen.

Boxes were stacked everywhere. On the window sill and against the cupboards, over the fridge and under the sink, peeking through an open cupboard door. They were plain cardboard boxes, and I reached for the one that was open on the counter.

Chocolate bars. It was full of chocolate bars. All in plain silver wrappers. There was no brand name. I took one and tore it open without asking and bit into creamy chocolate, crunchy wafer, heaven.

It was a genuine Farnsworth.

They were all Farnsworths.

"How?" I said, speaking through a mouth full of chocolate crumbs. Mrs de Menthe came and stood in the doorway and regarded me sadly.

"They're Eddie's, he keeps some of them here. I know it's not strictly legal, but it's only a bit of chocolate, Nelle. It doesn't harm anyone."

"No, I mean. . ." I stopped, the bar halfway to my mouth. "They're *Farnsworths*," I said.

"Are they?" She didn't seem bothered by my revelation.

"The factory has been shut for three years!"

"They do taste a little stale," Mrs de Menthe said.

I stared at the boxes. Was that possible?

I thought of my conversation with Detective Levene.

I thought of the elusive Mr Farnsworth.

And I felt the pieces of the puzzle finally starting to click into place.

22

The teddy. It kept coming back to the teddy bear. It was the link to Farnsworth, the proof of . . . what?

Find the teddy, and you'd find Farnsworth.

He was hiding in plain sight. *He* was Eddie's supplier. It was *his* chocolate that was sold at the playground, *his* candy that competed with the Consortium's. *He* was at the heart of it all.

He was still fighting the chocolate war.

How had I not realized this before? But I'd never tasted Eddie's chocolate. When Anouk offered me a candy bar at the playground I had turned her down. Everyone must have *known* Eddie had a stash of Farnsworth chocolate – everyone but me. Or did they? It still didn't answer the question of just *where* the chocolate was coming from. And *who* was giving Eddie a fresh supply. This was finally it, proof that my hunch was right, Farnsworth *was* still in the city. He was the key to this whole situation.

When I left Mrs de Menthe's apartment I exited the building to the same quiet neighbourhood and that same sense of watchful unseen eyes. When I went past the swings there was nobody there, though one was still swinging, as if it had been hurriedly and recently abandoned.

I heard a car engine coming to life, but I kept walking. I'd left my bike chained a short walk away. My heart was beating fast and I was relieved to see it was still there. I reached for the lock when the sound of the car engine roared close by, just behind the trees, and made me jump. A sudden siren blared, a screech that tore up the silence and uprooted it from its foundations.

"Fancy running into you again, Miss Faulkner."

"Detective Tidbeck," I said, forcing a smile. "What a pleasant surprise."

They climbed out of their car and came and loomed over me. Webber scowled.

"You've been poking your nose in a lot of places, kid," he said. "It's like everywhere we go about our lawful business, there you are. Snooping around . . . even bothering old Mrs de Menthe. She's very *anxious* we find her grandson, you know."

"Right."

"Talking to all *kinds* of characters," he said. "Unsavoury ones, if you don't mind me saying so. You been sticking your nose in our business, kid, and I don't like it."

"What business is that?" I said.

"Don't be cute." He glared at me. "We know you have it," he said.

"Have what?"

"The teddy. We want the teddy, kid. And we're through playing games."

I was through playing games, too.

"You don't want the *teddy*," I said. "You want Mr *Farnsworth*."

Tidbeck smiled, with those awful white teeth.

Webber, very slowly, clapped.

"Smart kid," he said.

"Find the teddy, find Farnsworth," Tidbeck said. "You follow?"

"I think I do," I said.

At least, I hoped I did. That teddy – it had to have been precious to Mr Farnsworth. I remembered the photo in the newspaper from his father's funeral. The way he held on to the teddy bear. Like it was the only friend he had in the world. Tidbeck was right, I thought. The teddy must have come from Mr Farnsworth himself – *he* must have given it to Eddie. It was the one concrete link to the invisible man. It was clearly important to him, and he would want it back. If there was a way to draw Mr Farnsworth out, the teddy had to be it. The one thing that would lure him out of the shadows.

And I was suddenly scared all over again. Tidbeck and Webber were taller and stronger than me, and they were *cops*. There was no sound but for the car engine and the blood beating in my ears.

"I think I want to go home now," I said.

"She wants to go home," Webber said.

Tidbeck hadn't said a word and hadn't moved. Then she smiled again, as though she'd just thought of a particularly unpleasant joke.

"Why don't we give you a ride?" she said.

"Yeah," Webber said. "Little girl like you on her own. It's not safe."

"I have my bike," I said. "It's fine. But thank you."

"We insist," Webber said. "Serve and protect, and all that."

"Just get in the car, Nelle," Tidbeck said.

Webber picked up my bike effortlessly and carried it to their car. He opened the trunk and folded the bike in, like he was putting a baby down to sleep. I looked at him and I looked at Tidbeck and I looked around, but I could see no escape.

"We just want to talk to you, Nelle."

"I don't have it!" I said.

"What was that?"

"I don't have it," I said. "I had it but it's gone. It's the truth. Honest."

"Ah," Tidbeck said, and she smiled again, a big tooth-fairy smile. "*Now* we're getting somewhere."

23

I sat in the back seat of the car. Tidbeck was in the passenger seat, looking out of the window. Webber drove, his fat fingers wrapped around the steering wheel. The car smelled of strawberry bubblegum and wet dog. There were takeaway boxes and empty soda cans on the seat and on the floor. I rolled down the window. The wind was warm. It was cool inside the car.

"Someone just brought you the teddy," Tidbeck said, "and then someone else stole it?"

"Basically, yes."

"And you don't know who or why?"

"No."

"If you hear anything," Tidbeck said, "*anything* . . . you will come to me. Are we understood?"

I thought about it. Webber hummed an old song, something about a golden ticket.

"Do I have a choice?" I said.

"Do you have to ask?"

"No," I said. "I suppose not."

"Good girl," she said.

My nails dug into the palms of my hands but I didn't say anything. Implied in her words were all sorts of threats. And I was still worried about Eddie. I had to find him before they did.

"You're trying to find Mr Farnsworth so you can shut down his operation," I said. "Right? Because his chocolate's competing with the Consortium's. Because he still *has* chocolate, and there's no chocolate like Farnsworth chocolate."

"I think little girls should keep quiet if they know what's good for them," Tidbeck said.

"I'm going to tell the mayor!" I said, with a sudden

burst of courage. "You're not going to get away with this!"

Webber barked a short laugh. "Don't you worry about the mayor," he said, and I saw Tidbeck elbow him painfully in the ribs.

"Ow!"

"Shut up, Webber," she said.

"What do you mean?" I said quietly.

It couldn't be that the mayor was involved, could it?

Tidbeck turned to me and smiled. "The mayor is a very busy man, Nelle. He has no time for kids' games. That's all. Right, Webber?"

"Right, right. That's what I meant."

We drove along as the city outside slumbered. The sun shimmered in a haze over the horizon. Dark birds huddled on tree branches and watched us pass. Webber hummed a song about a boat ride.

"Mr Lloyd-Williams said you came in with a teddy for him to look at, a few days ago," Tidbeck said.

"Yes."

"A Farnsworth."

It was too late for lying. "Yes."

"Do you know where Farnsworth is hiding?"

"No," I said.

Tidbeck turned away from the window and looked back at me.

"Are you sure?"

"Positive," I said.

"Because it would be a very silly thing to do, to keep something from me, Nelle. And you don't strike me as a silly sort of girl."

"Is that a compliment?"

She turned back to the window. Whatever she saw outside seemed to engross her.

"Your little friend is in a lot of trouble," she said.

"Eddie?"

"We really do want to help him, Nelle. It might not be too late."

"You won't hurt him?"

"Now, why would we do that?"

But she smiled unpleasantly all the same.

"All we want is the old man," Webber said.

"Bring us Farnsworth, and Eddie gets a pass from us," Tidbeck said. "Otherwise when we find him he's going to be in a lot of trouble. You think about that."

"All right," I said.

She nodded. Her nails drummed on the window.

I saw the library building just ahead.

"Can you drop me here?" I said. Then I saw the Sweetie Pies on the steps. I saw Tidbeck register their presence too. She exchanged a glance with Webber, who grinned in a mean sort of way.

"*Loitering*," he said, "with *intent*."

"Selling contraband in a public building," Tidbeck said.

"I think perhaps we need to do something about that," Webber said. "Being cops and all."

"Wait," I said. "What are you going to do?"

Webber smirked, turned on the siren and sped towards the library, braking with a screeching of wheels in front of the steps. The Sweetie Pies saw the car and tried to run. Webber jumped out and chased them, shouting. They scattered in different directions, though Little May turned back, just once, and threw a chocolate egg that hit Webber in the face. She screeched with laughter. Webber roared and lunged after her but she was too quick and too small for him to catch and he stopped a short way away and stood with his hands on his knees, breathing hard.

Tidbeck pushed the door open. We both got out of the car.

"Wipe that egg off your face, Webber," she said icily. He glared at her, but said nothing.

"I don't think those little girls will be back any time soon," Tidbeck said.

I figured she was probably right.

So much for the Sweetie Pies.

Webber ambled towards us, wiping his face.

"Can I have my bike?" I said.

He grunted but complied, taking it out of the trunk and dumping it on the pavement unceremoniously.

Tidbeck glared at me.

"The teddy," she said. Her voice was devoid of inflection. "Bring it to us."

She didn't say, *Or else*.

She didn't have to.

"We run this town," Webber said. "And we ain't playing games no more. You got that?"

He climbed back into his seat and slammed the car door.

"No games," I said. "Got it."

"Go," Tidbeck said quietly. Her voice was colder than ice cream. "We know where to find you."

And with that, they drove away.

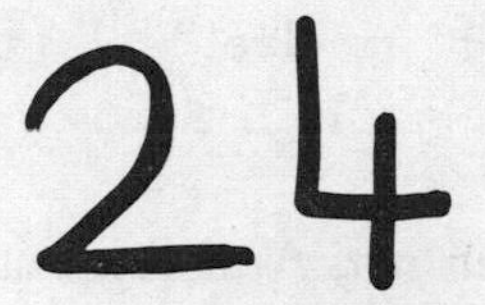

I entered the library.

I found Sweetcakes Ratchet in the far corner of the fiction section under "Crime". She had her back to me and her shoulders shook and it took me a moment to realize that she was crying.

I stood there, not sure what to do. Perhaps she sensed me, because she turned her head and glared.

"What are *you* doing here?"

"I was looking for you," I said.

Her face was blotchy and red from the crying. "It's not *fair*!" she said abruptly.

"What isn't?" I said.

"Eddie and Waffles and . . . and. . ." She waved her hand angrily. "This could have been *my* town!"

"You're only twelve!" I said. "You still have time."

"I'm almost *thirteen*! And I'm better than they are, I'm tougher, I could beat them!"

"Do you want to, though?" I said. I thought of Eddie, missing, and Waffles alone in his mansion on the hill. "Do you really want to live like that? Always being alone, always being afraid?"

"Oh, Nelle," she said, with a voice as bitter as grapefruit. "Perfect little Nelle. You think everyone's like you? Going around, poking your nose in things, always telling people what's right and what's wrong? Some of us have to live in the real world. It's not always great to be a kid."

"I know that!" I said, getting angry. "But what do you want, Mary? What do you *want*?"

"I want to be big!" she screamed. A solitary browser in the "Romance" section turned her head, then shuffled away. We were alone. "I want to be a grown-up, I want to do whatever I want, without people always telling me what to *do*!"

"But grown-ups just have even *more* rules," I said, frustrated. "They have to have jobs and pay bills and . . . and . . . stuff! They have to look after *us*!"

"Well, they're not doing a very good job of it!" she screamed, and then she started crying again, but quietly. The tears just flowed down her face as she stared at me.

"Mary. . ." I said.

"Leave me *alone*!"

I just stood there, feeling helpless. It felt strange, to see this bully I was afraid of, suddenly vulnerable. Suddenly crying.

"It's just not fair!" Sweetcakes said. "Everybody hates me. And I didn't even do nothing! And I had nothing to do with the fire in Mr Singh's store!"

Snot was dripping out of her nose. I searched for a tissue, didn't find one. She rubbed her nose on her sleeve and grimaced, looking at me miserably.

"What happened?" I said, quietly.

"I don't know!"

"But you were there," I said.

"Yes." She sniffed.

"You saw it?"

"I don't know what I saw. Some man."

"What man, Mary? This is important."

"Some man! Some skinny guy. He went past and then I saw he had a bottle in his hand and a piece of cloth twisted into the mouth of the bottle. He took out a lighter and he set the cloth on fire and then he threw the bottle through the store window. It broke the glass and it burst inside. It must have been full of gasoline. There were flames. They just . . . blew up. I never saw a real fire before."

She was no longer crying. I looked at the set of her face.

"Why were you there?" I said gently.

"I was watching the place, that's all. I knew Bobbie went for the pick-up." She snorted when she said it. "So we were gonna grab all the candy when his couriers showed up. Only this guy came along first and then I ran. I didn't know what else to do."

"Is that it?" I said.

"What do you mean?"

"Did you know this man? The one who started the fire?"

"Nah. Never saw him before."

"Why would he want to burn down the store?"

"I don't know. Maybe someone paid him."

And I thought, Tidbeck and Webber arrived on the scene of the fire awfully fast.

Almost as though they knew it was going to happen.

"What would you do if you won?" I said. "I mean, let's say you took over the candy racket tomorrow. Beat all the other gangs. You'd rule this town. You'd have all the candy you ever wanted. What then?"

She looked at me and she looked a little lost; and then she smiled, just a little. "I don't even like candy that much," she said.

When she smiled she was almost nice. I gave her my hand and, after a moment, she took it.

"Come on," I said. "Let's get out of here."

"Where?" she said. She looked so miserable that for a moment I wanted to laugh.

"To a party," I said.

"Sure, a party," Sweetcakes said. "Sure."

She looked away and then back at me, with haunted eyes.

"I'm sorry about, you know," she said.

I thought about the grief she'd given me at school, and in the case.

"I won't say it's all right," I said. "Because it's not. But I appreciate you saying it."

"See?" she said, with a hint of her old anger. "There you go again, being better than the rest of us."

"I'm not better," I said. "I'm really not."

"Well," she said, "I'm sorry, anyway."

She looked sincere. I smiled.

"Thanks," I said.

She stuck out her hand, awkwardly, for a shake.

"What do you say?" she said. "Start over?"

I looked at her proffered hand. I couldn't say Sweetcakes Ratchet was my favourite ever person, but you had to start somewhere.

Finally I shrugged, and took her hand.

"Sure," I said.

25

By the time we had arrived at the McKenzie mansion on the hill, the sun was just dipping into the sea, like a doughnut dunked into a bowl of blueberry sauce. I knew it was going to ruffle feathers, bringing Sweetcakes to Waffles's party, but I had had enough of the war between the gangs. It was time to call it quits.

The gates to the McKenzie place stood open and cars were parked on the street outside and in the driveway. They were big expensive cars driven by big expensive people.

Or, rather, by their chauffeurs.

The chauffeurs huddled in a group to one side of the gates. They wore black ironed uniforms and they were chatting in low voices, some furtively biting into forbidden chocolate bars. They were waiting for their employers, like nannies gathered at the gates to a playground as their young charges played inside.

Sweetcakes and I marched through the gates and to the side-gate for the gardens, which is where we encountered Gordon and Ronny, both dressed in black suits. Ronny's was too big and his hands disappeared up the long sleeves, while Gordon's was too tight and made him look like a choked penguin.

"What's *she* doin' here?" Gordon said.

"Yeah," Ronny said.

"She's with me," I said.

"With you, snoops? Who said you could bring a guest?" Gordon said.

"Yeah," Ronny said. He puffed up his chest importantly. Sweetcakes took a threatening step toward him and he cowered back, then pretended to look elsewhere. Sweetcakes barked a laugh.

"Get lost," I said. I was tired of playing games and tired of little boys playing goons.

"Boss ain't gonna like it," Gordon said, but you could tell the fight just wasn't in him.

"Oh, I *suppose* you can go in, then," Ronny said, knowing when to give up.

So we did.

When we got past them, we followed a trail lit by long torches planted into the ground. The air was perfumed with night flowers, lit by fireflies, alive with the sound of glasses touching. Grown-ups were talking and laughing, the sound growing louder as we approached the back of the house.

At the end of the trail stood a wooden arch garlanded with flowers. The butler, Foxglove, stood to attention, his hands gloved in white, his suit impeccable, his eyes still sad.

"Miss Faulkner," he said gravely.

"Hello, Foxglove," I said. He almost smiled.

"And who is your friend?"

"This is Swe— Mary Ratchet," I said.

"A pleasure, I'm sure," Foxglove said. Sweetcakes

scowled but seemed to decide he was being sincere, and subsided.

"Please," Foxglove said. "Welcome to the party. Waffl— I mean, the young master –" Sweetcakes snorted, and I had to hide a smile – "is currently indoors but shall emerge forthwith."

"Excuse me?"

"Shortly. I mean to say, very soon."

"Oh."

"Please help yourselves to the buffet," the butler said.

"We will," Sweetcakes said, and she marched through the arch, her boots crunching on the gravel, not waiting for me to follow her.

"Foxglove," I said.

"Miss Faulkner?"

"You know . . . do you know Eddie? Eddie de Menthe? He used to come up here a lot."

"Eddie, of course."

"He doesn't come here any more, does he?"

"No, I'm afraid not. He has not been seen on these premises for some time, Miss Faulkner."

"Do you think," I said, in a small voice, "that something bad happened to him?"

"I'm sure the young gentleman is perfectly fine," Foxglove said. "Wherever he is. He had always seemed to me like a most capable young man."

"Yes," I said. "I'm sure you're right, Foxglove."

"Very good, Miss Faulkner."

He stood aside, waiting for me to pass through the arch. I took a step, then stopped and looked at him. His sad eyes regarded me out of his expressionless face.

"Do you like chocolate, Foxglove?" I said.

When he smiled it transformed his whole face. For a moment even his eyes weren't sad any more, but bright and clear.

"Very much, Miss Faulkner," he said, in his soft, slow voice. "Very much indeed."

"That's what I thought," I said. I smiled back at him, and then I went through the arch and into the party, and left him standing there.

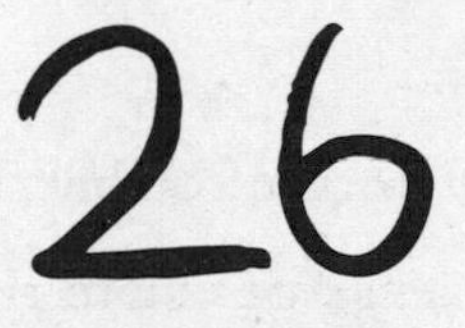

26

The night was lit with lanterns, scented with expensive perfumes and men's colognes. Soft music played against the hum of conversation and, at the far end of the pool, I saw the string quartet, two women and two men, all in tuxedos, their bows gliding across the strings as their reflection rippled in the water of the pool. Posters hung everywhere, with Mr Thornton's smiling face and the words, "Re-elect Thornton".

A long buffet table on the other side was laden with sweet pastries, chocolate and cream, in flagrant violation of Prohibition. They must have been brought in from out of town. I was shocked to see them there, but only for a moment. I'd already known not all grown-ups played by the rules – even if they made them.

I made my way uncomfortably through a forest of taller, bigger people, all of whom ignored me.

I looked for Sweetcakes and found her by the long buffet table, stuffing her face with cream puffs.

"There you are," she said. There was a ring of whipped cream all around her mouth. "This isn't so bad, is it, Nelle? When I grow up proper I'm going to go to lots and lots of parties."

No one seemed to mind that we were there. The grown-ups were clustered in groups, holding glasses of wine or champagne, talking and laughing as though their lives depended on it.

I turned at the tread of heavy footsteps, and a nasal voice said irritably, "What is *she* doing here, Nelle?"

"Waffles," I said, turning to him.

"You bring, her *here*? To my *house*?" His head moved from side to side like a toy's. "She's crazy, Nelle! She burned down my store!"

"Did not!" Sweetcakes said, indignant.

"It's all right, Waffles," I said.

"It's Mr McKenzie to you, snoops!"

I sighed. So we were back to that. I was getting tired of his attitude.

"*Waffles,*" I said. "Stop behaving like a spoiled brat and listen to me."

He looked at me in mute incomprehension. I don't think anyone had ever spoken to him that way before. He was a child used to always having his own way. I wondered how his parents had ever managed to wean him off diapers. Perhaps they never had. The thought made me smile.

"What are you smiling at?" Waffles said, rediscovering his anger. "Don't you smile at me! No one has the right to *smile* at me!"

"Shut up and listen to me, Waffles," I said. That made him open and close his mouth, but his voice dried out. "It's time to end this war, once and for all. Sweetcakes – Mary – didn't burn down Mr Singh's store."

He sneered. "Is she paying you?" he said. "Is that

it?" He waved an accusing finger in my face. "Is she paying you to say that? You brought her into my *house*, Nelle!"

"I want you to say sorry," I said.

"*What*?"

"And you too, Mary," I said, turning to Sweetcakes, who was watching the exchange with a smile of amused contempt.

"What?" she said. She dropped the smile but kept hold of a half-eaten cream puff. "I'm not going to do that! What for? I didn't do nothing!"

I looked at them glaring at each other. They looked so ridiculous that I almost felt sorry for them.

"Elmore," I said, using Waffles's first name, and Sweetcakes grinned. I glared at her and she stopped. "I want you to apologize to Mary for picking a fight with her and her gang and for accusing her of burning Mr Singh's store."

"I would never. . .!" he began, but I raised my hand, silencing him.

"Mary," I said. "I want you to apologize to Elmore for trashing Bobbie's place, which I *know* you did, because I was there, and also for trying to take over the candy racket."

"You can't make me!" she said. "I've got as much right to run candy in this town as this spoiled little rich kid!"

"Who are you calling a little kid?" Waffles said, puffing out his chest indignantly. "You think you're tough? I can be tough! I can be real tough!"

"You're as tough as a slice of cheesecake," Sweetcakes said. "Melted butter's tougher than you."

"Take that back!"

"Make me!"

"Stop it!" I said. I must have shouted. I saw the grown-ups turn and stare at our little group before looking away, uninterested in what they thought were kids playing. "Stop it, both of you! Stop acting like *children*!"

Waffles stared at me, and then Sweetcakes did too. I don't know what it was, maybe it was something in my face, but they both, first Waffles and then Sweetcakes, began to laugh.

They laughed like people who hadn't laughed in

a long time, so long they couldn't even remember what it felt like. Waffles laughed like a hyena, in short sharp barks, and Sweetcakes laughed with a big belly laughter that seemed to boom across the night. I felt my face turn red with anger and humiliation.

"Stop it!" I shouted. "Stop it!"

"Y-you . . . s-stop it, snoops!" Waffles said, laughing so hard it was a miracle his teeth didn't fall out.

"S-s-s*noo*ps!" Sweetcakes roared. Tears were streaming down her face. She clutched the side of the buffet table desperately.

"H-h-here," she said. "Have a . . . have a . . . have a *cream puff*, Nelle!"

And with that she turned – and shoved one right into my face.

I stood there, shocked, cream and pastry all over my face.

"You *didn't*," I said.

"She did!" Waffles screeched. I stared at him and Sweetcakes, still roaring at the sight of me. I couldn't help it. I felt it rise in the pit of my belly, and then it escaped.

A giggle.

And then another, and another.

I couldn't help it.

I started to laugh.

"S-s-she has c-c-cream all over her *face*!" Waffles shrieked. I was laughing so much it was hard to stand straight.

I said, "You think – you think that's – you think *that's* funny?" and I picked up a raspberry pie and hit him smack in the face with it.

Sweetcakes was rolling on the floor, her legs kicking in the air, laughing so hard that snot was coming out of her nose. The grown-ups were staring in our direction and moving away, not wanting to get any dirt on their smart party clothes. Waffles blew a raspberry and picked up a waffle heaped with syrup and cream.

He looked at me speculatively.

"Don't you . . . don't you *dare*!"

But I was laughing too hard. He threw it at me and I ducked, and it fell and hit Sweetcakes in the face. Then we were all three of us throwing pies, cream puffs and chocolate profiteroles at each other, shrieking like we were mad – which the grown-ups must have thought we were. I heard a gruff male voice say, "Elmore, stop that at once!" but it seemed too far away. A woman shrieked as a strawberry tart hit her in the face. The musicians faltered but then picked up again.

I was crawling on the ground by then. "S-s-s-stop it!"

My ribs hurt from laughing.

"Elmore, I am *ashamed* of you!" a woman said in a stern, angry voice.

"Somebody *do* something!"

"Foxglove? Foxglove! Where *is* that butler?" a man shouted.

The laughter was leaving me in small hiccups and when I looked around I saw Waffles in his ruined tuxedo, and Sweetcakes in her army coat covered in custard, and it threatened to start all over again, but I regained control of myself.

"Foxglove! Sort this immediately! Where *are* you, man?"

We stood up sheepishly, still giggling.

"Say sorry," I said.

"S-s-s-sorry!" They both threatened to burst out laughing again.

"Shake hands."

"She'll never stop, will she?" Waffles complained.

"She can be incredibly annoying," Sweetcakes said. "Trust me."

"Guess we better do as she says."

"Guess we'd better."

"You're all right, 'cakes."

"Guess you're not too bad, Waf."

They shook hands.

And suddenly, just like that, the candy-gang war was over.

27

I was getting myself cleaned up when I saw the flashing lights of the police car as it slid silently to a halt outside the McKenzie mansion. The doors opened and closed and Tidbeck and Webber strutted across the gravel. I watched out of the window from the second floor of the house. The big doors of the mansion opened and out stepped a man who went to welcome the detectives. He had a very familiar face.

I stared.

It was the mayor.

They disappeared inside. I hurriedly tried to wipe

chocolate off my shirt but only managed to smear it some more. I gave up and hurried out of the bathroom and on to the landing, just in time to see them passing by, down the stairs.

I tiptoed after. The thick carpet swallowed the sound of footsteps. I saw their backs as they disappeared down a long corridor.

I followed.

Elderly McKenzies stared down at me with pursed lips and disapproving eyes, but they were only old portraits and I did my best to ignore them. I saw the mayor and the two detectives disappear into a large room with a long oak table in the middle. I crept to the door. It had been left very slightly ajar. Very carefully, I pushed it open the tiniest bit more, so I could look inside.

"Well?" the mayor said irritably. "Did you find it?"

"Sir, we're actively looking," Tidbeck said. "There have been some unfortunate setbacks—"

"I don't get the whole thing with the teddy," the mayor said. "Are you sure it is going to lead you to him? Are you sure it's not just a red herring?"

"A fish, sir?" Webber said. "I'm pretty sure it *is* a teddy."

"Not a fish, you idiot. A *red herring.* Something that looks important but turns out not to be all that relevant."

"I don't really like fish, sir."

"Oh, for . . . never *mind,*" the mayor said acidly. He turned on Tidbeck, already dismissing Webber from his mind.

"Time is running out, detective. I need to find that man! *I want that factory!*"

I stared in horrified fascination as the mayor spoke.

I had suspected the connection before, but I hadn't wanted to believe it to be true.

But it was really him.

It had been the mayor all along.

I stared at him, there in the room, giving orders.

But what I couldn't understand was . . . *why*?

"We don't yet know where he's hiding, sir. He could be anywhere. For all we know he was at this party!" Tidbeck said. "However, we have to assume the teddy will draw him out. We know it is precious to him."

"Then why did he let it go in the first place?" the mayor said.

"We think he gave it to the boy, de Menthe. His *protégé*."

I knew that meant something like "an apprentice". Is that how Eddie got the teddy? It was passed on to him from Mr Farnsworth?

No wonder the two detectives were after Eddie, then.

No wonder he'd had to disappear.

"Then where is the boy?"

"We don't know. Yet."

"You find it! Them! I will suffer no more excuses!" He sighed. "Setting fire to that shop was stupid."

I held my breath when the implications of what he had just said settled in.

"You two have been skimming too much off the kids' candy. I do not care for candy! I never have."

"Yes, sir."

"Go out there and find them! Turn every stone. Do *not* let me down!"

"Yes, sir."

I watched them through the crack. Then I realized they were heading out and I flattened myself against the wall, my heart thumping. They didn't see me behind the door.

"We'll go have another little chat with Bobbie," Tidbeck said. "And then I think we need to put more pressure on that annoying little girl, Nelle. She knows more than she's letting on. It's time to end this."

Webber sniggered. I waited, frozen, until they were gone.

I should have left, but curiosity got the better of me. I came round the door and saw the mayor, still inside the room, gazing out of the window, his back to me. I went in.

Standing against the wall I saw a box of clear glass, with a picture above it.

The picture showed an aerial photo of the abandoned chocolate factory on the hill. It showed just how immense it really was.

The factory sprawled in all directions, like a miniature town all on its own. There was a series of interlinked halls built in brown brick, with immense

towering chimneys rising from the flat rooftops. There were shining pathways woven between the buildings, where tiny people moved in tiny carts.

Below the photograph, encased in the glass, was a model of the same area, but the factory was gone. In its place rose a development of shining new homes, with neat manicured lawns and white picket fences, a playground to one side, even an artificial lake.

A small note beside the display said, "Proposed plans for area redevelopment".

I stared at it in fascinated horror. Which is when the mayor turned his head and saw me.

For a moment he looked irritated. "Where did you come from?" he said.

"I was looking for Waffles," I said. "I mean, Elmore."

"Ah, the McKenzie boy," he said. "Well, he's not here."

"You're the mayor," I said.

I knew his face, of course. I'd seen him on TV a few times, and at the rally I'd seen him from a distance. Now, though, he was standing right by me, so close I could reach out and touch him. He had a thick shock of black hair, a close-set mouth, a chin that jutted out just a little bit. He wore black-rimmed glasses with round frames and he smoked a pipe. He wore a shabby suit. You wouldn't notice him if you passed him on the street or in the shop. He was just a man.

And yet he wasn't. He was Mayor Thornton.

"I see you are admiring my project," he said. He turned to look at the model under the glass.

"Beautiful, isn't it?" he said.

"It's . . . but . . . but the factory!" I said.

"Oh, that horrible old thing has to go, kid," he said. "It has no place in the modern world."

"But the chocolate—"

"Disgusting stuff. Trust me, kid. We'll make this city great again. It will all be for the better."

"But Mr Farnsworth!" I said. I couldn't help myself.

"Farnsworth? Farnsworth!" he said. "Don't you worry about *him*, little girl. He's nothing but a joke." There was no more warmth in him any more, if there ever was. "I don't like jokes," he complained. "I never get them."

He saw my face. "Don't worry," he said. "It will all be over soon. It's just a formality, really. Just a matter of doing the paperwork."

"Paperwork?" I said.

"The title deeds," he said. "I just need that awful Farnsworth man to sign them over to me. Which he will, just as soon as I find him . . . but like I said, little girl, don't you worry about *that*."

Then he smiled, a practised public smile with little kindness in it. "Here," he said. He handed me a button with his face on it and a legend that said, *Thornton for Mayor.* "Does your mommy vote? You'll give it to her, won't you? Remember, always eat your greens, and Vote Thornton!"

He patted me on the head and then glided away, already forgetting me, our conversation, the minor irritant I must have seemed to him.

I stood there, watching him go. I stared at the model of the proposed new development where the chocolate factory still stood.

So *this* was what it was all about. He was going to make Mr Farnsworth sign over the factory – he was going to *force* him to!

I swore right then that I wouldn't let him get away with it.

There *had* to be a way to bring him down.

28

I ran. Outside I could hear the police siren as Tidbeck and Webber sped away from the mansion and down the hill. I needed a *telephone*! I kept running into grown-ups as their party was winding down. I finally found Waffles upstairs.

"Waffles! Where's the phone?"

"Hey, Nelle, have you seen Foxglove? Only he's disappeared and no one can find him." He looked really distressed. "Nothing really works without him."

"Forget Foxglove!" I said. "Where's the telephone?"

"There's one over there," he said, pointing. I ran

to it, picked up the receiver, started dialling Bobbie's number. The wheel dial went *whirr . . . whirr . . .* and I said, "Come on, come on!" until at last I had dialled all the digits and the phone made a dialling tone.

It rang a few times but at last someone answered.

"Hello?"

"Mrs Singh! I thought you were in hospital."

"Nelle! I was." Even over the phone it sounded like she was smiling. "I couldn't keep away, seeing what trouble my two boys got themselves into."

"I'm so glad you're feeling better. Is Bobbie home?"

"It's nice of you to call," she said. I heard her calling beyond the phone. "Bobbie? It's Nelle!"

He came on the phone. "Hey, Nelle."

"Hey, Bobbie. Listen, Tidbeck and Webber are on their way over to you. I think they were the ones who burned down your store. You need to get out!"

"I don't care about that any more," he said. "I'm out of the candy biz, Nelle. I'm out for good."

"And after that they're coming for me!" I said.

"Then just stay out of their way," he said. "What do you *want* from me, Nelle? I told you, I quit the game."

"Is that what it is?" I said, angry. "Just a game?"

"Of course it isn't!" I could hear him breathing. "My place was burned down. My dad nearly got killed. It's not worth it, Nelle. Give it up! Walk away. You keep poking your nose into things that don't concern you. You could get hurt."

My hands balled into fists. I felt furious. After everything, to be warned away by Bobbie was just too much.

Then I realized how much scared he was, and my fingers relaxed and I said, "I'm sorry."

"Nelle . . . it isn't *your* fault," he said gently.

"I know it isn't, Bobbie!" I said. He was quiet, on the line.

I said, "You know I can't stop now."

He hesitated.

"I know," he said.

Then he said, "You better go. I think I can see them coming."

I cycled down Sternwood Drive as fast as I could. I'd bought myself some time but I had to find Mr

Farnsworth somehow – I had to *warn* him! I reached home and jumped off my bike and went into my bedroom to pack up essentials. I was going to find out the truth.

The house was dark. My mom was out. I was all alone.

Back in my room I put on dark clothes and comfortable shoes and packed a flashlight. I was on my way out the door again when I caught a glimpse of something shiny under the table. I kneeled down to look, then picked it up.

I stared at it.

It rested in the palm of my hand.

It was a shiny glass marble.

His little head poked out of the door when I knocked and when he saw me he smiled with that same trusting smile he always gave me. I waited as Cody stepped out into the yard between our houses.

"Hey, Nelle," he said.

"Hey, Cody."

"What you got there, Nelle?"

"It's a marble, Cody."

"I like marbles," he said.

"I know."

He looked at me, with those eyes full of trust.

"Why did you do it, Cody?" I said.

"Do what, Nelle?"

"Steal Eddie's teddy," I said.

His little face fell and he looked at me almost in reproach, as though I'd hurt him.

"I *didn't* steal it," he said.

"Come on, Cody."

"I didn't! I was just . . . it was so lonely just sitting there on the shelf, in the playground, and I didn't think anyone would mind."

"Wait," I said. "You stole it from the playground *first*?"

"Well ... yeah."

This wasn't what I had expected at all.

"So you just *took* it?"

"Yeah. It was easy."

He looked down at his feet.

His confession took me by surprise. But, thinking about it, things suddenly made a lot of sense.

"I didn't think anyone would mind," he mumbled.

"But people did," I said. "Lots of people did."

"Yeah. I told Eddie! I gave it back to him."

"You *did*?" This was not what I was expecting, either. Little Cody was just *full* of surprises.

"Sure. But then he got worried and I think he went to your house and left it for you. I think he figured it was safer that way. He had to go away for a while."

"And then, what, you came in to my *house* and took it again?" I said.

"I had to, Nelle! I had to look after it. I didn't think you'd mind, really."

"Well, you dropped your marble when you came in," I said.

"You keep it," he said. "Here." He took out a handful of marbles from his pocket and put them in my hand. I didn't know what to say. I put them in my pocket so as not to hurt his feelings.

"I'm so sorry," Cody said. "I never meant to—"

"I know," I said. "I know."

Abruptly he gave me a hug. I held him in my arms, feeling how little he was.

"It's all right, Cody" I said awkwardly. I stroked his hair.

He released me and again gave me that beaming, trusting smile.

"I was just keeping it safe," he said.

"Can you get it for me?" I said.

"Sure."

He went inside and when he came back he was holding the teddy.

I took the bear from Cody. It stared at me affectionately with its one good eye.

It was the Farnsworth teddy bear, all right.

I hugged it close to my chest.

"You'll look after him, won't you?" Cody said.

"I will, I promise," I said.

"OK, then," he said, and he looked relieved. "Eddie did say I shouldn't have taken it."

"*Eddie* said that? When?"

"After I took it."

"After you took it the first time, or the *second* time, Cody?"

He looked at me in confusion. "Does it matter?"

"Yes, it *does*, Cody!"

"The second time. After Eddie gave it to you to look after."

"But . . . you mean you *spoke* to Eddie *after* he'd disappeared?"

"Sure. I mean. . ."

He just shrugged. I took hold of him by the shoulders and held him gently, but not so gently that he could escape if he wanted to. "Listen to me carefully, Cody," I said. "*Where is Eddie*?"

He glanced up and I followed his gaze. He was looking towards the hill. And I knew then that my hunch had been right all along. That Eddie would be hiding in the one place no one would go looking for him.

In the chocolate factory.

But I had gone round it, and the whole place was locked tighter than a prison, the gates closed and the walls high and no way in. . .

I stared into Cody's eyes.

"How, *exactly*, do you get into the chocolate factory?" I said.

He smiled, like it was obvious, and he was only wondering why I'd ever needed to ask.

"Through the sewage pipes," he said.

29

"Ewww!" I said.

We were somewhere down the hill. The vast open mouths of cylindrical copper pipes jutted out of the hillside. They emerged into the air above our heads. A trickle of dirty sewage water dribbled down and joined the flow of other pipes. The water ran out and down to the sea. The smell was disgusting: it was like rancid butter and boiled fat and dirty diapers, spoiled eggs and burned carpet and vomit and cheese.

There were . . . bits, floating in the water.

I tried not to see what they were.

"I thought. . ." I said, trying to talk while holding my nose. "I thought the factory was closed."

"Yeah?" Cody said.

"So why is there . . . stuff coming out of the pipes?" I said.

Cody shrugged. I looked at the water coming out of the pipe. It had an oily sheen. The other pipes were for domestic waste. There were no other factories nearby.

"Come on," Cody said. He began to climb. There were grey-white stones set into the steep slope, and he held on to them and used them to propel himself up.

He moved quickly and easily. I followed reluctantly.

The smell changed when we reached the main pipe. It still smelled bad but it was more familiar. It had hints of cocoa butter and coconut and ground coffee beans. The water was only in the bottom of the pipe and it was a light brown colour.

It was dark inside the pipe. I held the flashlight and followed Cody.

In moments, the light of the moon disappeared, and the mouth of the pipe was gone as though it had never existed. It was very dark, and I could hear things moving through the water ahead of us. Cody's little face looked anxious but he led the way. As we progressed deeper into the hillside, the pipe curved and it became harder to walk. I tried to hold on to the walls but they were slimy, and I said, "Ewwww!" again, and hurriedly wiped my hands on my jeans.

"Shhh!" Cody said. He stopped and stood still, and I froze beside him.

"What?"

"Shhh!"

I listened. Then I heard it.

At first I mistook it for the beating of my heart. But then I realized the sound was real.

DUM.

It vibrated through the pipe. It rang up through the soles of my feet and travelled up my legs.

DUM.

The sounds travelled down the pipe and made the water tremble and shake, and when I pointed the flashlight down, it showed me my own reflection shivering in the circles of water.

DUM.

DUM.

DUM.

DUM.

Then it was over, as suddenly as it began. The silence returned but there was something terrifying about it, worse than the sound of the—

DUM.

"It was just the pipe," I said, trying to convince myself.

DUM.

"A machine thumping on the pipe or—"

DUUUUUMMM!

I jumped. The sound reverberated through the pipe and made my teeth hurt. The water splashed and shook violently.

"We have to go back!" Cody said.

"We can't!" I said. "Cody, let's go. Take my hand."

"No, Nelle. Come back with me—"

DUM DUM DUM DUUUUUMMM!

I couldn't stop him. I didn't want to. Cody bolted, back the way we'd come. I shouted after him but the sound of my voice was swallowed in the increasing din.

"Oh, no!" I said, out loud.

DUM! *DUM*! *DUM*! *CRACK*!

I looked down at my feet. The water level was rising. The flow was increasing rapidly.

I began to run. Not back. Ahead. I had to, even though I knew it was crazy to do it. I ran through the pipe as fast as I could, my feet landing in the rapidly-rising water. The thrumming of the pipe intensified. It was all around me, and the distant hum was that of machinery: the *CLANG-THWAK-WHIRR* of giant engines.

They were coming alive.

I heard the roar of distant water. My feet *SPLISH-SPLASH-SPLOSHED.* The flashlight fell from my fingers and was lost in the current. The water was up to my knees, and rising.

The walls were slimy and there was nothing to hold on to.

The rush of the water came closer and closer. I pushed forward helplessly. I wasn't going back. I couldn't.

The water rushed towards me. It would pick me

up and throw me like a rag doll: like garbage. It would slam me against the sides of the pipe and push me back, back along the sewage pipe, all the way to the ocean.

But I couldn't give up.

Then I saw it.

A glimmer of light ahead. I pushed forward faster now.

There!

The pipe split into two sections in the distance. Two dark mouths waiting – but I thought I saw a weak, flickering light just coming through in the distance inside one of them. I pushed against the water, breathing hard. The water wasn't cold but it felt slimy and gross. Floating in the water were broken coconut shells, torn burlap sacks, bits of string. Everything smelled of oily, rancid butter.

I wasn't going to make it.

Everything became about the next step, and the next, and the next.

DUM.

DUM.

DUM.

DUM.

CRACK!

I dove.

There was water in my eyes and in my hair and I couldn't see. I was lost in a dark river, and for a moment I didn't know which way was up, which way was down. Then I opened my eyes, and the glimmer of light was still ahead, through the left pipe, and I kicked and my foot connected with the wall and slid but I *pushed*, my arms reached out and *swept* back – and I was suddenly free.

I fell through water into cool blessed air. I flopped down on the floor of the pipe as the flow of water grew to a roar, and a flood burst through the right-hand pipe, entirely flooding the place where I had just been. I scrabbled away but I was higher than the water, and I was safe: just very wet, and very sore.

I lay there like a landed fish and watched the water surging through the pipe. I heard the clang and thrum and beat of engines coming alive, some in the distance, some closer by.

And I realized the factory was waking up all around me.

After three long years, it was coming alive.

I pushed myself up and looked ahead, where the light beckoned. I walked to the end of the tunnel. It must have been an engineer's path, to access the sewers. I knew I was close, then, close to the heart of it all.

At the end of the tunnel was a small, ordinary wooden door.

I pushed it open.

I emerged into starlight and a warm wind on my back. The door I came through was set into a large square brick building. The sign on the door said, *Sewage Treatment – No Unauthorized Access* in faded script.

I was somewhere at the back of the factory. I could just see the side-gate entrance in the distance, and two loaders rusting in the open air.

The outer buildings were dark: but in the centre of the factory grounds stood the largest building of them all, a vast and imposing brick cube with small windows set high up. A blazing light shone out of them, illuminating the sky, almost erasing the moon entirely with its radiance.

It was the manufacturing floor, the heart of the chocolate factory.

It was where the magic happened.

I walked towards it, drawn to the light. I felt the hum of machinery under my feet, a constant thrum that reverberated through the ground.

As I walked I saw the whole of the factory spread around me, the vast block-like buildings that had sprung up and been added to over the years since the first small shack (or so the story was always told me) was built at the back of the Farnsworth house, all that time ago. It was the story of humble beginnings, of a simple love of chocolate somehow transformed into a business empire. The truth was probably a little different. These buildings were old, they were built to last.

This had always been a factory.

Far in the distance were the main gates, and before them was the great courtyard, where the workers assembled every morning. It was the size of a football field, and it was empty. Nothing moved and nothing breathed.

Nothing but me.

I walked to the main building. I tried the doors but they were closed. I circled it, feeling the intensity of the machines inside rise, the thrum of power under my feet, in my teeth, on my tongue. It made my hair stand on end.

Then I found the side entrance. I tried the door.

It opened.

Somehow, I knew that it would.

I stepped inside.

And on to the main production floor.

The ceiling rose high overhead.

Underneath it, I felt as small as though I were standing in a vast cathedral. The light shone down and everywhere I looked, I saw the machines.

Alive now.

Burping and warbling, shaking and rattling.

Mixers and centrifuges, roasters and temperers and refiners and kibblers, ovens and coolers and coaters and wrappers!

The machines churned out chocolate. Perfect blocks plopped down on to the assembly lines and ran on to the far end, where they were automatically wrapped and packed, and the boxes were piled high against the wall.

I stared all around me, everything else forgotten, for the moment. The world smelled of chocolate again. It smelled of milk and almonds, of strawberries and vanilla. It smelled of peaches and raspberries and orange blossom. It smelled of bubblegum and mint and baked wafers. It smelled like the world smelled back when it was perfect.

"It's beautiful, isn't it?" a voice said. I realized I had shut my eyes.

I knew that voice.

I opened my eyes.

Waffles McKenzie's butler had his shirt-sleeves rolled up and he was chewing on the end of a chocolate cigar. He regarded me with those sad large eyes. I realized they were the colour of chocolate, and wondered why I'd never noticed that before.

Eddie stood beside him.

"Miss Faulkner," the butler said, in that soft, sad voice.

"Hello, Mr Farnsworth," I said.

31

I was drying out next to a vast oven. Steam rose from my clothes. The air was scented with baked pastries.

"It was you," I said. "All this time it was you."

The butler and Eddie were playing cards, betting chocolate coins. Eddie was winning. He gave me a sheepish grin but kept his eyes down. He knew I was angry. He'd dragged me into all this, and while I was running around trying to solve the case he was hiding all the while.

Foxglove – Mr Farnsworth – cradled the sodden teddy in his arms. He stood and paced, the cards forgotten. He was both like and unlike the butler had been. He looked the same, but now he moved with barely suppressed energy, and there was a new, determined set to his mouth.

"Thank you for bringing back my teddy bear," he said.

"It was my fault," Eddie said. "I shouldn't have got you involved, Nelle."

"Do you have any idea of the trouble you've caused?" I said. I was almost shouting.

"I didn't mean to get you in trouble," he said. He looked contrite. "Nelle, I didn't have a *choice*! They were after me, but to them I was just a kid, and you're just a kid. The only one they really wanted was Mr Farnsworth."

"You," I said, turning on the former butler, pointing an accusing finger.

"Yes, Miss Faulkner."

"Don't Miss Faulkner me!" I said. "You were there, all the time! You were hiding in plain sight? As a . . . a *butler*?"

"It's a profession with a long and most respectable

tradition," Mr Farnsworth said. "But you knew, didn't you? You knew already, before tonight."

"I suspected it," I said. I thought about it all, finally putting everything together. "You helped Waffles set up his gang. Why? To fight Prohibition? But you were just helping the Consortium!"

"The enemy of my enemy is my friend," Mr Farnsworth said softly. "And besides, how else would I know what they were planning? I had to be close."

I said, "As a butler, you could watch everything going on and no one even knew you were there."

"No one ever suspects the butler," he said, though he had the good grace to look sheepish when he said it.

"Nelle. . ." Eddie said.

"No! And you!" I said. "He helped *you*, too, Eddie, didn't he? *He* supplied you with candy. Old surplus chocolate bars, so you could become this big-time gangster. You weren't even a bootlegger, not really – you didn't have to smuggle anything *into* the city. It was already here."

"They raided the factory," Mr Farnsworth said, "but they never found the old cellars. I'd been running extra batches for months beforehand, knowing the day would come. Not wanting to believe it, but preparing for it nevertheless. I stored away everything."

"And you could go in and out through the sewage pipes," I said.

"Yes."

"It was easy. And no one would ever know, because everyone knew the factory was shut down. Abandoned. Empty."

"Yes."

"You know the truth of it, Nelle! I am the victim of a great conspiracy. The Consortium –" he all but spat the word – "those hacks! Those faux-chocolatiers! Assassins! Murderers! I never wanted anything but to make people happy, by making candy. Candy *is* happiness, Nelle. And they took it away from me."

"You don't *understand*!" I said, almost shouting. I was wasting time, interrogating him, and he didn't even *know*. "It isn't the Consortium, it isn't about the candy, even – it's about the *factory*, Mr Farnsworth."

"What *about* the factory?"

"Mayor Thornton wants to tear it down! He wants to build new homes on it." I took a deep breath.

"He wants the *land*, Mr Farnsworth," I said. "*That's* why those detectives from Prohibition have been looking for you all this time."

Mr Farnsworth stared at me, his mouth open in shock.

"He would never!" he said. Then his eyes narrowed and his face hardened in a way I didn't like. "Well, he cannot have it. He will never have it! I—"

He was going to say more, but right then there was an almighty crash in the distance and his eyes shone and his lips tightened to a line.

"They're *coming*," he said.

I stared at the factory, lit up like a birthday cake. No *wonder* they were coming, I thought. Mr Farnsworth had made sure they would.

Eddie made distressed faces at me.

CLANG! *CRASH*! *BANG*!

And I realized it was the main gates. They were being battered down.

"Miss Faulker," Mr Farnsworth said. He was the

dignified butler again. "Thank you again for returning my teddy. You had better leave now. I do not wish to place you in danger."

I stared at him in disbelief.

Mr Farnsworth looked at me sadly. As though he could somehow read my mind, he said, "Making friends has never been easy, for me."

I nodded. There seemed nothing to say. The gates groaned in the distance. They sounded like they were weakening.

"Goodbye, Mr Farnsworth," I said.

"Goodbye, Nelle."

He turned. His back was to me. It was as though he had already forgotten I was there.

I looked at Eddie. Eddie looked worried.

Mr Farnsworth began pressing buttons on a big control panel.

"Eddie, what is he doing?" I said.

"He knew this could happen," Eddie said. "He made *plans*."

"What kind of plans?" I said. "We have to get out of here!"

"No! I'm not leaving!" Eddie said. "Mr Farnsworth is going to reopen the factory. He's already making new candy, Nelle! He's never going to give the factory to Mayor Thornton! Never! You'll see. Everything's going to be all right, Nelle!"

I wanted to hit him. Then I realized that despite the tough-seeming exterior, underneath it he was just lonely, and scared.

"I promised your grandma I'd bring you back," I told him gently.

CRASH! *GROAN*. . .

THUD.

We looked at each other. Mr Farnsworth strode across the platform and disappeared from view, going down the metal steps to the production floor.

"Eddie, we need to get out or we'll be in a *lot* of trouble!"

Something in my tone must have penetrated into his thick skull because he nodded. I took his hand in mine. It was dry and warm. We ran to the stairs. We heard a car in the distance, coming close, not hurrying. It stopped outside the building and the engine stilled.

I heard two doors open and shut.

I heard two sets of footsteps on the hard, dry ground.

It was too late for us to run.

"Hide!" I said.

"Where?" Eddie said.

I pulled him by the hand, behind one of the glass vats where pink bubblegum mass pulsated as it grew and expanded. The pink mass pushed against the glass. I stared at it in horrified fascination.

It seemed almost alive.

"We know you're in there, Farnsworth!"

The shout rang through the vast hall.

It was Tidbeck's voice.

Webber laughed cruelly.

"Hide-and-seek, Mr Farnsworth!" he said. "Hide-and-seek. You're it!"

From behind the machine I could see only their feet.

Tidbeck's black shoes, shined to perfection.

Webber's boots, with spatters of mud.

They were still, waiting.

For a moment there were no human voices. The machines alone talked, thumping and churning, making more and more candy. Then a cold, clear laugh cut through the air. It came from all the corners of the hall at once. It made my hair stand on end. It rang clear as an icy bell, pure as snow. I saw Webber take a step back, heard the slither of metal on leather, the snicker of a gun safety being cocked.

Eddie grabbed my hand. We looked at each other. We were both scared now.

"Come on out, Mr Farnsworth!" Tidbeck called. But her voice had lost its conviction. It sounded thin and alone in the hall. "This isn't a game!"

"Oh, but it *is*," Mr Farnsworth said – and his voice came from right behind the two detectives. I stuck my head around the machine for a better look. Both detectives swung round at once, guns pointing – but there was no one there.

"It's his public announcement system," Eddie said beside me. "He can watch, and talk to, every part of the production floor. He said they took away his workers, but they couldn't take away the machines – so now the machines can do everything themselves. All he has to do is press the right buttons."

At that moment the bubblegum machine we were hiding behind made a high-pitched, sickening whine. The raw bubblegum mass blew outwards, splattering the sides of the glass. I took Eddie's hand in mine and we began to run.

"What was th—" Tidbeck started to say, and the glass casing exploded.

Glass fragments shot through the air, falling on the floor with a sound like rain. I couldn't help it – I turned to look. A mass of pink goo exploded out of the machine, and globs of sticky raw bubblegum fell everywhere, splattering against the walls and on the floor.

I saw Tidbeck half-turn, her arm raised – and a mass of bubblegum came down on her in a giant splatter.

She screeched in rage. She was almost swallowed by the mass. She tried to fight it, but it stuck, and as it did it began to solidify, responding to the air, so that Tidbeck's movements became slower and slower.

"Get me *out* of this!" she screamed. Mr Farnsworth's disembodied voice laughed coldly all around us.

Webber cursed and came to Tidbeck's help. From somewhere he brought out a knife. He scraped the pink bubblegum off her as best as he could.

When she could move again, she was furious.

"That was a big mistake, Farnsworth," she said. Eddie and I had scampered up one of the low platforms above a wafer press. Large wafer squares emerged out of an oven and were chopped precisely and pressed down on to flavoured fillings. From there we could see everything.

Tidbeck marched towards the centre of the room like a gunslinger from an old movie. The gun was in her hand. She had blotches of pink all over her face and clothes.

The conveyor belts continued to move, endlessly carrying bars of chocolate. Tidbeck knocked them aside contemptuously. Chocolate fell on the floor and broke, dirtying it. Mr Farnsworth howled through the unseen speakers.

Tidbeck smiled.

Then she raised her gun, closed one eye, took aim high overhead and pulled the trigger.

32

The gunshot echoed through the room. High above, a vat of chocolate milk exploded.

Milk rained down everywhere, and with it came shards of glass. It splashed the machines and dribbled on the floor and created a brown waterfall that fell down in sheets and turned into a tepid lake when it hit the floor.

Mr Farnsworth howled again, unseen.

"I could do this all day!" Tidbeck screamed.

An alarm began to wail, somewhere in the distance. Webber sauntered towards the wrapping machines. The chocolate kept coming. Webber pulled off a long metal bar with a screech of groaning metal. He hefted it in his hands and smiled. Then he attacked the wrappers.

Sheets of beautiful paper tore and ripped. Webber's arms rose and fell in a blur of motion. Bits of wrapping paper flew everywhere, rising on unseen currents, dipping and rising like butterflies, drifting to all corners of the factory. Webber howled with glee. Tidbeck took aim with her gun again and squeezed the trigger, and a mound of multi-coloured lollipop-hard sugar exploded.

"Ow!" Eddie said. He touched his cheek and when he took his hand away there was something sticky and red on his finger. He put it in his mouth.

"Hey, it's sweet," he said, surprised.

He'd been hit by a sugar shard.

"Stop!" Mr Farnsworth screamed.

"Come out!" Tidbeck shouted. "You are under arrest!"

"I will destroy you!" Mr Farnsworth said. "How *dare* you, come over here, to *my* place, *mine*! You think you could take it from me? I have done nothing but bring people *joy*! This is *my* chocolate factory, this will *always* be a chocolate factory! How dare you, you. . .?" Words failed him.

Tidbeck smirked.

"Who are you going to tell?" she said. "There is no one here, Farnsworth. No one here but us."

She raised her gun again and fired, and another tank of milk exploded high overhead.

"Mayor Thornton sends his regards!" Tidbeck screamed.

Mr Farnsworth howled again on the public announcement system. The sound filled the whole of the factory, a cry of terrible anguish and distress.

"Come out or this will go badly for you!" Webber shouted. He rested with his hands on the metal bar. He was breathing heavily, his face red. Bits of wrapping paper fluttered everywhere in the air. Dirty chocolate mud covered the once-pristine floor. Gum and candy shards were splattered against the walls. "Come out and we can be merciful, Farnsworth! Ain't nobody here to help you!"

Beside me, Eddie did something very stupid.

"No one here but *us*!" he shouted. He stood up very tall. Or, at least, as tall as he could. I was still taller than him, just about.

Both Tidbeck and Webber turned and looked in our direction. Tidbeck's face warped in an ugly sneer of recognition. Webber just looked angry.

"Come over here, kids. You don't want to get *hurt*," Tidbeck said, with an awful, sugary sweetness in her voice.

"Oh, Eddie, no!" I said, horrified.

"What?" his pale freckled face was turned to me. "Look what they're *doing*!" he said. "We could be witnesses, wc could tell everyone, they'd have to believe us, they'd—"

Everything happened kind of fast then.

Firstly, Webber came after us. He didn't run so much as lumber, the metal bar still in his hands. I looked around helplessly, then my eyes aligned on the ladder leading up to the higher ramps.

I pulled Eddie after me and we began to climb. My palms were sweating and it was hard to hold on to the rungs.

"Come down from there, kids!" I heard Webber shout. When I finally reached the top ramp I leant down to help Eddie up. Behind his mop of red hair I could see the whole factory floor spread wide below us. Webber was directly underneath us now, trying to climb but having trouble. He kept cursing and hitching his belt up, but eventually he began to follow.

"Hurry, Eddie!"

I pulled, and he collapsed on the metal floor beside me. I saw Tidbeck looking this way and that, her gun out, her eyes searching. There was no sound from the public announcement system. Then I heard an engine roar to life. Tidbeck turned and turned, wildly, trying to find the source of the sound. Webber had almost reached the level we had just vacated.

Then I saw it.

It was one of the golf buggies they used to use in the factory in order to get around.

It had the Farnsworth colours.

It had an open top.

It had Mr Farnsworth, grinning maniacally, behind the wheel.

The cart's headlights shone ahead, catching Tidbeck in their beams. She turned, one hand raised to shield her eyes, the other still holding the gun.

The golf cart, with another roar of its engine, sped and ploughed straight into her.

I screamed.

Detective Tidbeck was knocked aside by the impact. She rolled and the gun fell from her hands and slid fast across the floor. Farnsworth whooped in triumph and began to turn the cart. Tidbeck pulled herself up, her face a furious mask of pink bubblegum and dirty chocolate milk.

"We have to do something!" I said.

"What!" Eddie said.

Below us, Webber was still reaching for the rungs on the ladder. He looked up at us and smiled an awful smile.

"Well, *do* something!" Eddie said.

Then I remembered the marbles Cody had given me. I'd forgotten about them, but they should still be there. . .

I reached in my pocket and my fingers closed around them.

I pulled them out. Looked at them in my hand.

Then dropped them down on Webber.

His feet were still on the ramp. The marbles bounced with a gentle chime. Webber looked surprised. He tried to change position – and slipped on the marbles.

He fell like a sack of cookie dough.

There was a heavy thud.

Then silence.

When I looked down I saw that he was lying peacefully on the ground. He wasn't moving.

I was very quiet. I climbed down the ladder and stepped carefully over the ramp and the marbles, and slid down the rest of the way.

Eddie followed.

We stood over Webber. His chest was rising and falling evenly. He was breathing.

He still had that surprised look on his face.

"Whoa," Eddie said. "His head's gonna be real sore when he wakes up."

"You think?"

I felt shaky but I didn't have time to worry about Webber or what I'd done. Just ahead, Farnsworth had turned around and the little golf cart's fender was aimed straight at Tidbeck again.

She stood, shaky but upright, and the gun was back in her hand. She must have scrambled for it while we were busy dealing with Webber. It was dripping with dirty chocolate water.

Her face was a frozen mask of hatred, as if she'd bitten on a bitter lemon peel.

"Stop!" I shouted. Neither of them paid me any attention.

Farnsworth revved the engine.

Tidbeck sighted along the barrel of her gun.

I began to run.

I didn't know what I could do. I only knew that I had to try.

Dimly, I was aware of other noises, the sound of wheels crunching gravel, distant shouts. I was too slow, I'd be too late.

"*Stop*!"

Everything moved too fast and too slow.

Farnsworth pressed the accelerator and the cart sped towards Tidbeck.

He smiled.

I heard the scream of a police siren outside, short and sharp.

Tidbeck began to squeeze the trigger.

I ran straight and threw myself at her.

Her arm went wide. The shot rang through the hall. Tidbeck turned furiously, the gun in her hand, swiping at my head.

I ducked – just barely. I felt the whoosh of air where her arm passed. Instead she grabbed me by the hair painfully, and *pulled*.

"You think you can take *me* on, you little—" she said.

The cart hit her sideways, missing me.

Detective Tidbeck fell back and as she did her finger tightened on the trigger again and the gun fired.

The sound was an explosion, making my ears ring.

The air filled with the smell of gunpowder. I shook my head, trying to clear it.

Then I saw Mr Farnsworth.

He was thrown back against the seat of the cart, looking winded.

Tidbeck collapsed on the floor.

The cart rolled, and then stopped, and Mr Farnsworth lolled out of his seat.

I stepped over Tidbeck and ran to Mr Farnsworth. He looked up at me and tried to smile.

"I just wanted to ... make candy," he said. "It always made ... *me* happy, when I was a ... child."

Distantly, I heard the police siren again, and shouts, and running feet. Then Detective Levene was there, standing above us, and hands were reaching down to pick Mr Farnsworth up. He reached for my hand.

"You won't let them ... take it all away from me, will you, Miss Faulkner?"

I looked into his eyes. "You need to get to hospital," I said gently. His eyes were full of anguish. Then he nodded, and smiled again, and they lifted him up and took him away.

"Detective Tidbeck?" I heard Suzie Levene say. She kneeled beside Tidbeck's prone body. She held handcuffs. "You're under arrest for bootlegging, extortion, corruption, wilful destruction of property, intimidation and attempted murder." She cuffed

Tidbeck's hands behind her back and helped her to her feet. "Anything you say or do may be used against you in a court of law. Do you understand?"

"What?" Tidbeck said. She looked stunned. "What?"

I turned. Webber was being led away by other police officers.

"But how did you know to come here?" I said.

"Hey, Nelle."

I turned and Bobbie Singh was smiling at me.

"Hey, Bobbie," I said, and I was smiling too.

"After you called, I went to your house. Just to make sure you'd be all right. I was just in time to see you and Cody head up to the factory. And I thought to myself, I thought, I bet Nelle gets into trouble," he said. "I wasn't wrong, was I, Nelle?"

I watched Mr Farnsworth being wheeled away. Eddie was with him, keeping pace with the gurney. Detective Levene led Tidbeck away in handcuffs.

Through the open doors I could see the flashing lights of the police cars, and the beginning of a new dawn in the sky. Inside, the factory was finally silent.

Broken glass and spilled milk and torn paper lay

everywhere. The machines burped out one last bar of chocolate and fell silent. The chocolate bar rolled towards us along the slowing conveyor belt, until it came just within reach, and there it stopped.

I reached over and broke a piece off and put it in my mouth and chewed it.

It tasted delicious.

"No," I said. "No, I guess you weren't."

33

In the early hours of the morning, after everything that had happened in the chocolate factory, Detective Levene drove me home.

My mother was waiting outside.

Her face was pale and tense. There were black rings under her eyes. When I stepped out of the car, she ran to me and took me in her arms and hugged me so tight I thought I'd burst.

"Don't you *ever* do something like this again!" she said, when she finally released me.

Then she grounded me for six weeks.

I slept what was left of the night and late into the morning. My sleep was deep but when I woke the sheets were crumpled, as though I had tossed and turned the whole time. Several days later I went back to my office, and looked at the photo of me and my dad outside the factory. I felt sad for a while, and then I hung it carefully on the wall and went back to the house and I felt better.

I tidied my office. I read books. I rearranged all the cutlery in the drawer. I sorted the fridge. I watched television.

"Please can I leave the house?"

"No."

"*Please* can I leave the house?"

"No!"

I made my mom breakfast. I helped bring in the shopping.

I even watered the garden plants.

"Hey, Nelle."

"Hey, Cody."

His little face peered over the fence.

"I didn't mean to cause so much trouble, you know," he said. "It's just, he was such a lovely teddy bear."

"I know, Cody."

"I'm sorry."

"It's all right, Cody."

He smiled happily. "They say soon you'll be able to buy candy again," he said. "In the store."

"Who says?"

He shrugged. "They do," he said.

"You need to lay off the candy," I told him. I must have said it a hundred times.

"I know," he said. "I don't eat so much any more, Nelle."

"Really?"

"Swear," he said. "'Sides, Mom got me a computer. With games and everything. I'm playing all of them. I'm in training. I'm gonna be a champion, Nelle. A world champion."

"That's good," I said.

He beamed at me. "Yeah," he said. "Well, see you, Nelle."

"See you, Cody."

Sweetcakes came to visit a few times. She brought with her news of the outside world. "Your mom's being awful harsh," she said, munching on an oatmeal cookie. "*Oats*," she said, and made a face. She gathered the crumbs in the palm of her hand daintily.

"It's not so bad," I said. "Have you seen Eddie?"

She scowled. "That little runt," she said. "I wouldn't pick my teeth with him."

"So you have?"

"He's around. Back living with his granny." She barked a laugh. Cookie crumbs flew. "He's not running candy no more, though. The biz is finished. There ain't no candy *anywhere* on the streets. All the kids are going crazy. They'll get over it." Her eyes turned dreamy. "It was good while it lasted, though."

Waffles called once.

"Snoops?"

"Waffles."

"Yeah. So listen—"

"I'm listening."

"Just wanted to say thanks. You know?"

"What for?"

"For everything, really. But for, you know. Helping Foxglove, in the end. I mean, I know that wasn't his real name or anything. And I guess he wasn't really a butler. Only he was to me. And he was my friend. I don't have too many friends."

"No," I said. "Neither did he."

There was an awkward silence. Then: "Well, I just wanted to say thanks. And if you ever need a favour, you just let me know. I owe you one, snoops."

"OK," I said. "Thanks."

"Laters, snoops."

"Laters, Waffles."

Detective Levene came to visit, once. She sat very straight in a chair with a cup of coffee balanced in her lap. My mom and I sat on the sofa opposite.

"The city would like to thank you for your part in taking down a dangerous bootlegging operation," Detective Levene said, "and for exposing certain members of the Prohibition Bureau who may have been . . . remiss in the carrying out of their duties."

"Remiss?" I said.

Detective Levene looked hard at the coffee cup in her lap.

"*Remiss*?"

"Detectives Tidbeck and Webber have voluntarily resigned from the force," Detective Levene said.

"What do you mean, resigned?" I said. I felt anger rising. "They should be in jail!"

"Voluntarily resigned." It was like she was reading a pre-prepared speech. "To pursue new avenues."

"What does that mean?"

I may have been shouting. My mom put a restraining hand on my arm.

"Detective Webber left the force and is no longer in the city. He said something about going on a long fishing trip. He won't be back."

"Fishing!"

"And Detective Tidbeck has accepted a job offer in Bay City. Security consultant to the St Creme-Egge Corporation."

"So they get off completely free?" I said. "They don't even go to trial?" I balled my hands into fists. "And what about the *mayor*?"

Detective Levene and my mother exchanged glances. "Mayor Thornton has resigned from his post," Detective Levene said. "He will not be seeking re-election."

I stared at her.

"And that's *it*?"

I was still shouting.

"Sorry, Nelle," Detective Levene said. I could see she wasn't happy either. "Sometimes the bad guys get to walk away."

"But that's not *fair*!"

"No," she said gently. "No, it isn't."

After she'd gone, my mom made me a mug of hot milk and we watched television in our pyjamas. I was still feeling angry.

"Maybe you could go out tomorrow," she said.

"No," I said. "I'm still grounded, aren't I?"

"Well, maybe you've had enough," my mom said. "Also, someone keeps rearranging everything in the fridge. It's beginning to drive me crazy."

I almost smiled, but I didn't. I kept staring at the television. My mom stroked my hair.

"It's just not *fair*," I said.

"I know, Nelle. And I know you care. That's why I love you."

"You *have* to love me. I'm your *daughter*!"

"That too," she said, and she tickled me, and I laughed.

After Mayor Thornton resigned, one of the local council members ran unopposed in his place.

One of her first acts as the new mayor was to formally abolish Prohibition.

After three years, candy was legal again in the city.

And Bobbie got his wish.

Three months after that night in the factory, we went to the grand reopening of Mr Singh's Emporium.

"Thank you all for coming," Mr Singh said. He stood before the assembled guests, smiling nervously. He was usually a man of few words. Mrs Singh sat near her two boys, and she beamed at them.

Behind him, the chrome counter shone. A new soda fountain glimmered. Multi-coloured lollipops, each the size of a peacock's tail, fanned the wall.

Popcorn crackled in a stove-top popper. On the counter, rows and rows of Farnsworth chocolate bars in bright shiny wrappers stood, waiting.

Mr Singh cleared his throat.

"Well," he said, into the expectant silence. "Here it is." He spread his arms, encompassing the shop. Bobbie stood beside him.

Mr Singh put his arm around Bobbie's shoulders and they both beamed at the assembled guests.

The speech was over. Everyone clapped. We milled around. We bought chocolates. I ate a strawberry ice cream.

"Hey, Nelle."

I turned and there he was. Eddie, looking at me sheepishly, chewing on a candy bar.

"Hey, Eddie."

He wasn't so cocky any more. He stood there shifting his weight from foot to foot, with his red hair sticking out above his head, grinning in a way that made him look slightly lost.

I couldn't stay angry with him. Not really.

"I had a postcard from Mr Farnsworth the other

day," Eddie said. "He's in a sanatorium in Switzerland. He says he's recovering well. He asked how you were."

"I'm good," I said.

"Right. Right. Good."

"Yeah."

We stood there facing each other awkwardly.

"I'm sorry. And I never thanked you. For, well, everything."

"Hey," I said. "I brought you back the teddy, didn't I?"

I smiled. He smiled.

"Friends?" Eddie said.

I hesitated. Then I stuck my hand out, and we shook.

"Friends," I said.

Character Profiles

Nelle Faulkner

- Age: 12
- Role: Private Detective
- Likes: Justice; fairness; a nice slice of cherry pie
- Dislikes: Mysteries
- Motto: "Do the right thing, whatever the cost"

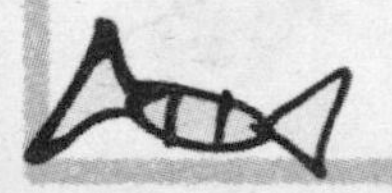

Eddie de Menthe

- Age: 12 and a half
- Role: Candy smuggler
- Likes: Chewing gum; his grandmother
- Dislikes: The long arm of the Law
- Motto: "Trouble is my business"

Bobbie Singh

- Age: 12
- Role: Informant
- Likes: Order
- Dislikes: Mess
- Motto: "Just when I thought I was out, they pull me back in"

Mary "Sweetcakes" Ratchet
Age: 12 and a half
Role: Bully
Likes: Nothing
Dislikes: Everything
Motto: "Give me that!"

Elmore "Waffles" McKenzie

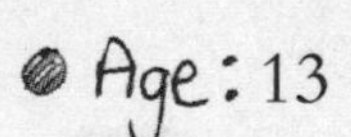

- Age: 13
- Role: Candy gang boss
- Likes: Waffles; hot chocolate with marshmallows
- Dislikes: Carrots
- Motto: "No cake is too big, no cake is too small"

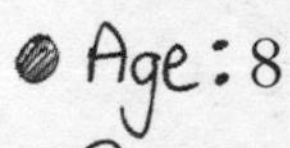

- Age: 8
- Role: Expert marble player
- Likes: Video games
- Dislikes: Loud voices
- Motto: "What's a motto?"

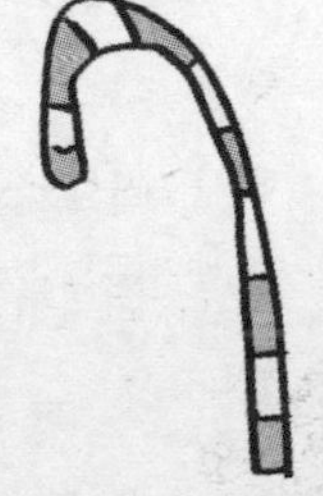